FINAL DESCENT

A NOVELLA

AUDREY J. COLE

RAINIER
PUBLISHING

© 2025 Audrey J. Cole

ISBN: 979-8-218-78385-3

ALSO BY AUDREY J. COLE

CHAPTER ONE

I CAN'T BELIEVE I'M doing this.

It feels ridiculous, sitting here at almost forty, waiting for someone I've never met. I look around the busy downtown restaurant and contemplate getting up to leave when my phone chimes with a new message. I swipe my phone off the table, thinking it's from my date.

But it's from Becca. *How's it going? Does he look like his photos? ...or did you get catfished?* A winky face emoji appears beneath my best friend's words.

I glance at the entrance before typing my reply. *He texted saying he's running late. I'm still waiting.*

Her response appears seconds later. *Well, if he's a no show, feel free to come over. I have tequila.*

I start to reply that I'm still not drinking, something Becca should know after everything that's happened.

"Claire?"

I'm startled by the deep male voice coming from the other side of the table, and my phone tumbles from my fingers.

"Sorry." My date grins, bending over to pick my phone off the ground.

Our eyes meet as he hands it back to me, and I'm already planning what I'm going to tell Becca. He's even hotter in person. My stomach does a nervous waltz.

"I didn't mean to scare you," he says. "I'm Evan."

"I'm Claire." I stand from my seat.

Even though I'm wearing three-inch heels, he stands a head taller than me. We exchange a quick hug that feels a mix of awkward and exciting.

"Thanks for meeting me." He takes a seat across from me. "Sorry I'm late."

"No problem." I take in his wavy brown hair and dark blue eyes, which remind me of Superman. He's obviously the same guy from his dating app photos, but they really did not do him justice.

When he lifts the menu, his bicep protrudes from the sleeve of his polo shirt. I force myself to scan the entrees so he doesn't catch me staring.

I sit back against the chair, shoulders relaxing. Maybe this wasn't such a bad idea after all.

He glances up from the menu. "You said you've been here before, right? What's good here?"

My phone chimes with a new text from Becca. I glance at the screen, sensing my date following my gaze. *Well?? Is he there yet? I need details!*

I drop the phone into my purse, ignoring her message. "If you like seafood, their fish tacos are really good. But I think I'm going to get the seasonal salad."

He motions to my ice water. "Are you getting something else to drink?"

I shake my head. "Not tonight," I say, not wanting to explain my recent stint in court-ordered rehab after the accident.

A waitress approaches our table. "Can I get some drinks started for you two? Or are we ready to order?"

Even though she refers to us in the plural, her gaze is fixed on Evan. She looks straight out of college, a good fifteen years younger than me, reminding me of my ex-husband's girlfriend, who's fresh out of nursing school. Her tight, low-cut T-shirt accentuates her large breasts, which are practically popping out of her shirt right at my date's eye level.

Evan nods at me. "You go first."

"I'm going to do your seasonal salad."

"Anything else to drink besides water?" The waitress keeps her gaze glued to the small notepad she's scribbling on.

"No, thanks."

"And for you?" She edges closer to Evan, pushing a long strand of blonde hair behind her shoulder before dropping the notepad to her side. Without it in the way, her breasts are inches from his face.

Evan looks up from the menu, keeping his gaze fixed on me. "I'll have the fish tacos. I hear they're amazing."

I bite back a smile.

"And to drink?"

"Just water, thanks." Evan holds my gaze as the young waitress scoops our menus off the table.

"You got it," she mumbles, the flirtatiousness gone from her voice.

Evan folds his hands on the table. "So, have you been on the app for a while?"

"No. Actually, this is my first date since my divorce. It's

been a year." I take a drink from my water. "I wasn't ready to start dating until now. I was in a car accident right after we separated, with my daughter." An image of Olivia lying in the ICU hospital bed, fighting for her life after the accident I caused, assaults my mind. "I mean, she's fine now, and I'm still not sure if I'm ready to date, but my therapist thought it would be a good idea." I cough when the water hits the back of my throat. *Oh, crap. Did I really just mention my therapist a few minutes into our first date? What is wrong with me?* I meet Evan's gaze, expecting him to be cringing. But his expression appears surprisingly understanding.

"Sorry," I add. "I'm not sure why I added that last part."

"Don't be. I was married once too. It was years ago, but I was devastated at first when it didn't work out. I saw a therapist afterward too. It really helped me get through it and get over my initial fear of being alone."

As his blue eyes seem to search mine, I shift in my seat, surprised at the instant connection I'm feeling with a stranger on a first date.

"We didn't have kids though, which made it easier, I think." The side of his mouth upturns to a smile. "I bet you're a great mom."

I force a smile. *No, I'm not.* Steven's words when I woke up in the hospital echo through my mind. *Where's Olivia? I* asked him. *Is she okay?*

No, she's not okay, Claire. You damn near killed her!

"And you're an airline pilot?"

Evan's question tears me from my thoughts.

I nod. "Yep."

"That's so cool."

"And you're in graphic design?" I ask, recalling what I read on his dating profile.

"That's right." He shrugs. "It's not exactly my dream job, but it pays the bills."

His phone rings, and he shifts in his seat to retrieve it from his pocket. He checks the screen and frowns. "Sorry. It's a work call. I should probably take this. Do you mind? It'll just take a second."

"Of course." I take another drink from my water as he answers the call and gets up from the table.

I watch his stride as he zigzags between tables and steps outside. His dating profile said his age is forty-two. How is this guy still single? I glance around the restaurant before digging inside my purse for my phone, trying to contain a smile as I type a reply to Becca.

He's here. And he's HOT. So far so—

"Sorry about that." Evan sits down and scoots in his chair. I lower my phone. "It's fine, really."

"I just started a big project for a super needy client. He's been calling me a few times a day and wants to throw around new design ideas even though I've already started working on what we agreed upon." He shakes his head. "Anyway, tell me more about you." There's something in his intensely blue eyes that keeps me from looking away. Like he sees something in me that no one else has noticed.

"Oh." I tuck a piece of hair behind my ear. "Well, there's not much to tell." Especially when you skip the part about crashing my car with my daughter in the back and nearly killing her. And my court-ordered rehab and mental breakdown that followed after Steven was temporarily awarded full custody. Thank God I have her back half the time now, even though that still doesn't seem like enough. "Um…I'm a single mom, as you know. Olivia is five. She just started kindergarten this fall."

I'm about to ask about him when our waitress returns, setting two plates on the table.

"That was fast," I say when she slides my salad toward me.

"I said *no* cilantro," Evan says, his voice taking on a cold tone.

"Oh," the waitress says, her smile fading. "I didn't hear that, or I would've—"

Evan slaps his palm on the table, rattling the silverware and making me flinch. The room falls quiet. He glares up at her, eyes going dark, as if he's morphed into someone else. I stiffen against my chair. It's a split-second transformation I've seen in only one other person. Steven.

The waitress takes a step back. "No, I—"

"One thing." He holds up a pointer finger. "That's all you had to remember. One. Damn. Thing."

He pushes the plate to the edge of the table. My mouth falls open, and the waitress grabs the plate before it falls to the floor. I didn't hear him say no cilantro either, but I doubt saying so will help.

"I'm sorry." She looks to be blinking back tears. "I'll have them make you a whole new entree."

"Don't bother." He waves a hand as if swatting a fly. "I've lost my appetite. Just take it away."

I feel a rush of sympathy for the young woman. From her stricken expression, it's taking all she's got not to cry. Holding the plate of tacos, she turns for the kitchen without a word.

He's a manchild, I think. *This* must be why he's still single. Evan returns his attention to me, his face softening to what it had been before our food arrived, as if nothing had happened. "Can you believe that? It's that Gen Z age group. It's like they've been raised by social media, can only communicate through text, and none of them know what the hell they're doing, you know?"

"Hmm." I feign a neutral expression, not wanting to argue with him. Whatever point he was trying to make, it still doesn't justify how he treated her. I'm glad now that I hadn't hit "send" on my text to Becca. Guess Becca won't be getting such a great report after all. I consider throwing a few bills on the table and getting up to leave. But I hate being rude, and the scene it might cause. Instead, I lift my fork and hurry to eat my salad, ready for this date to be over. But after a few bites, my stomach is in a knot. I set the fork down and put the napkin on the table.

"I guess I'm not that hungry anymore either."

"I hope I didn't ruin your dinner." Evan reaches for my hand across the table.

Instinctively, I pull mine away. "Actually, I'm not feeling that great. I think I may need to go home." I look around for our waitress to ask for the check, but she's nowhere to be found. Probably sobbing in a back room.

"I'm sorry if I came off harsh." He runs a hand through his thick hair. "It's something I'm working on...my temper."

Harsh? You came off like an asshole with a serious anger problem. But I keep that to myself. "No, it's not that," I lie.

"I'll get the check."

"Oh, you don't need to—"

"Excuse me." Evan taps a lanky waiter on the arm as he moves past our table. "Could we get our check please?"

"Sure," the man says. "I'll be right back."

I intertwine my fingers together on my lap, annoyed I took my therapist's and Becca's advice to get on that stupid dating app. I'm starting to understand how women end up murdered by some creep they met online. Thankfully, the waiter returns quickly with the check and hands it to Evan.

"You didn't charge me for the tacos, right?" Evan scans the bill.

The waiter trails Evan's gaze. "I don't believe so."

"Okay good." Satisfied, Evan snaps the bill folder shut and hands it back to the man along with his credit card.

I reach for my wallet, not wanting this guy to think I owe him something. "I can pay for my salad."

"No, I got it," Evan says.

I decide it's probably best not to argue. "Thank you."

"Be right back," the waiter says.

My hope of getting out of here soon deflates when I see the waiter stop at a neighboring table.

"So, what's it like being an airline pilot?"

A wave of revulsion travels through me at the idea of having to sit here any longer with this jerk. I should just get up and leave. I'm not a prisoner. But after seeing how Evan reacted to the cilantro, I'm afraid he'd cause another scene. Out the corner of my eye, I see the waiter running Evan's card behind a counter at the far wall. It will only be a few minutes, I tell myself, and we'll be out of here. Thank goodness I brought my own car.

"It's cool, I guess. It was my dream to fly planes for as long as I can remember. It's still a job, but I'm grateful that I get paid to do something I love." I stop myself before going on, knowing I talk too much when I'm nervous.

An awkward silence falls over us as he stares at me from

across the table. Maybe he's waiting for me to ask more about him, but after seeing his behavior with the waitress, I can't bring myself to fake interest.

"Thanks, you guys." The waiter returns and places the bill on the table in front of Evan. "Have a good night."

"Thank you," I tell him as Evan signs the bill.

I'm out of my seat before he sets down the pen.

"Hope she wasn't expecting a tip," he says, following me as I weave through the tables toward the door.

When I step outside, I inhale a breath of cool autumn air, happy this horrible date is almost over. Soon, I'll be in my car, driving away from Evan.

"Are you feeling well enough to drive home?"

I turn to find Evan right behind me. The sky darkened during our brief time inside. The city lights catch the sharp angles of his face.

"I'm happy to take you," he adds. "We could come back to get your car tomorrow."

He studies me with what looks like genuine concern. Does he really think I want him taking me home after he brought our waitress to tears?

"I'll be fine. Thanks anyway."

He walks beside me along the downtown street. When we near my Range Rover, I start the engine with my key fob, grateful I got a spot close to the restaurant. It strikes me that if I'm going to continue online dating, having an exit plan will be a necessity.

"Thanks for dinner." I pick up my pace without turning around. "It was nice meeting you."

"Can I get a hug?" Evan asks when I step off the curb.

I turn. Evan is already holding out his arms. Behind him,

an older couple enters the restaurant. I choke down a mental image of Evan plunging his dinner knife into my neck. *Stop overreacting. You're being crazy.* That's what Steven would say.

Just hug him and then you can go home. Reluctantly, I step forward and allow him to envelop me in his muscular arms. I get a whiff of his cologne, a mix of pine trees and citrus, when he pulls me against his chest.

As soon as he lessens his hold, I back up to make sure he doesn't go in for a kiss.

"Goodnight, Claire." He smiles. "Thanks for a wonderful evening."

I'm already off the curb, rounding the back of my SUV for the driver's side.

"Text me when you get home," he calls.

"Will do," I lie.

I climb inside and throw it into drive. As I pull onto the street, the *click* of the automatic locks is like music to my ears. Out the passenger window, I catch Evan getting into the black BMW that had been parked in front of me.

That's strange, I think. I'm almost positive that car was already there when I arrived. *It was probably another BMW,* I reason. *And it doesn't matter now.* I sink against my seat, relieved that I'll never have to see him again.

CHAPTER TWO

"That's a shame," Becca's voice resounds through the Bluetooth. "Why do all the super hot ones turn out to be assholes?"

"I'm starting to think I'm a magnet for men who are assholes."

I pull into the parking lot of Olivia's school. I'm early, thank goodness. Traffic can be unpredictable, and I can't afford to be late. Steven has made it clear that he doesn't think I'm a fit parent, and he'll use anything and everything to regain full custody.

Lakeview Elementary is only ten minutes from Steven's surgery office and his home in Bellevue. Since he had full custody of Olivia at the time of her kindergarten enrollment, she goes to school in his school district. Being one of the wealthiest zip codes in the state, the closest home I could afford on my copilot salary is thirty minutes south, longer in traffic.

"Everyone has a bad date story, right?" Becca says. "I'm sure your next one will be better."

"I've already deleted the dating app."

"What?" Becca's voice goes up a few decibels. "No, you can't do that. This was just one bad date. You can't give up already. It's good for you to get back out there."

I throw my car in park but leave the engine running. Gazing out the windshield, I'm relieved I don't have to pick Olivia up from my old house and see Steven's twenty-two-year-old live-in girlfriend's car in the drive. Seeing her social media post after Olivia was released from the hospital while I was admitted to a psychiatric facility only pushed me deeper into a downward spiral. *So glad our baby girl is home safe* was captioned below a selfie of the three of them on my leather sectional.

"I'm not *giving up* on finding someone. Just meeting someone online. Who knows? Maybe I'll meet someone at work."

Becca laughs. "You going to come back and help me serve drinks in first class?"

"I'm serious. Maybe I'll meet a widowed captain. Or I'll meet someone at the grocery store."

"The *grocery store?*"

I smile, envisioning the shock on Becca's face.

"It's not the 1950s, Claire."

"I gotta go," I say, seeing the time. Cars are starting to line up in the pick-up lane. In the parking lot, a few parents are getting out of their cars and walking toward the sidewalk that will soon be mobbed with elementary kids.

"Okay. But when we get to Boston on our layover next week, I'm taking you out. We'll hit up a bar and have some fun. I'll be your wing woman, and you can find a guy the old-fashioned way. Like it's 1995."

I stifle a laugh, imagining my friend who's been married

for nearly two decades as my wing woman. "I'll talk to you later."

I end the call and get out of my car, excitement traveling through me to see Olivia and have her through the weekend. When I reach the pick-up area, more parents are trickling in. I wait beside two moms I don't know who are deep in conversation about which dance studios are the best. More parents arrive, and the bell rings. The side door to the school opens, and students file out, bounding over to their parents.

I scan the children for Olivia, not seeing her or recognizing any of the other kids from her class. She must still be lined up inside, waiting to come out. The two moms next to me leave with their daughters in tow.

"Excuse me," one of them says as she brushes past me.

A tall, dark-haired man comes to stand a few feet away from me. He's wearing sunglasses, but I recognize him immediately. My heart drops into my stomach. It's Evan, my date from last night. Here. At my daughter's school. As I stand frozen, he looks my way and smiles.

"Mommy!" Olivia wraps her arms around the top of my legs.

"Hi, sweetheart." I glance over my shoulder as I return her tight hug.

Evan is still standing there, watching us in silence. *Does he have a kid at the same school?* My heart thuds against my rib cage as I remember his comment about his divorce, how he didn't have kids with his ex. *What then? Has he been following me?*

I think back to last night when a dark BMW sedan drove slowly past my house. I was getting out of my car, and the light wasn't great, but for a fleeting moment, I feared Evan had followed me home. Until I watched the car pull into a drive at the end of my street.

"I missed you." I take her hand and force a smile when she pulls away. "Let's see how fast we can get to the car. Ready?"

She beams. "Ready."

Keeping hold of her hand, I check for cars and dash across the parking lot. Olivia giggles beside me as her backpack bobs up and down, thinking this is a fun game.

My pulse is still racing when we get to the Range Rover.

"That was fun," she says as she buckles herself into her booster seat.

"Yes, it was," I lie. "How was your day, sweetie?" Before pulling out of the parking lot, I check my rearview mirror.

Evan hasn't moved from the pick-up area, but he's looking our way. I touch the gas to turn out of the parking lot as a mother holding her toddler steps in front of my SUV. I slam on the brakes.

"Watch out!" the woman yells as my head hits the headrest.

She scowl-gapes at me. "What the hell?" she calls before continuing past my car.

I hold up a hand in apology even though she's no longer looking at me. "Sorry."

Hands trembling, I pull into traffic while Olivia wonders out loud how worms breathe if they don't have noses—something she and Logan talked about on the tire swing. Fear wedges itself in my throat like a hard, unmoving rock.

What the hell was Evan doing at Olivia's school?

CHAPTER THREE

"**A**RE YOU SURE it was him?" Becca asks, sitting cross-legged on my couch.

I can still hear Olivia's bedtime music drifting down the hall. Just as I was tucking her into bed, Becca showed up on my doorstep. The voicemail I left her after seeing Evan at Olivia's school probably sounded completely unhinged.

"I'm positive." I don't tell her that Evan had sunglasses on. I can tell she's looking for a way to fix this, explain it away.

Becca runs a hand through her long, auburn hair. "I don't understand. How would he know where Olivia goes to school?"

"Maybe he followed me." I tell her about seeing a dark BMW crawl past my house last night.

Becca looks deep in thought, her gaze lingering on a framed photo on the wall of Olivia and me at Alki Beach two summers ago. "But you said the car pulled into your neighbor's driveway."

"Yes, but I didn't wait for anyone to get out." I pace in

front of the coffee table. "Maybe he did that so I wouldn't think it was him."

Becca traces a finger around the rim of her mug of tea, thinking this over. "Or maybe he had a reason for being at the school."

I stop pacing and shake my head. "He said he doesn't have kids, Becca. What if he's dangerous? What if he hurts Olivia?" I motion to the closed door to her room at the end of the hall. "How could I have brought some psycho into our lives?" A familiar weight of guilt creeps over me.

"This isn't your fault," Becca says, reading my expression.

I cross my arms, dropping my gaze to the floor. "Maybe I should tell Steven. He'll be picking Olivia up from school on Monday." More likely, his girlfriend will be. But still, if this guy is stalking me—and our daughter—he should know.

Becca uncrosses her legs and sits tall. "You can't do that. He'll use it against you. Blame you for bringing someone dangerous into Olivia's life." She sets her mug on the coffee table. "Don't you have this guy's phone number? You could ask him why he was there. Maybe there's an explanation."

"I deleted his number from my phone. And our texts."

"You could get back on the app. Send him a message."

I bite my lip, thinking it over. "Maybe." But what if that's what he *wants* me to do? I worry giving him any attention might make this whole thing worse.

Becca stands, tugging down the hem of her sweatshirt over her leggings. "While you're thinking about it, I have to pee."

After Becca disappears down the hall, the whump of a car door closing out front startles me. I move to the front window and push aside the curtains. My breath catches at the sight of the dark sedan parked on the curb. A tall man moves around the front of the car. The hood of his sweatshirt is pulled over his head, but the glow of the streetlamp one house down gives me a good look at his frame—tall and muscular. It's Evan. He leans against the passenger door and stares straight at me.

I recoil from the window, then move to the front door, making sure it's locked.

"Becca," I call.

No response.

I rush down the hall and bang on the bathroom door, pausing only when I hear Olivia shift in bed, then settle again.

Becca flings open the door, her eyes wide. "What?"

"It's him," I breathe. "The guy. He's out front. I just saw him through the window."

Her brows knit together. "Are you sure it's him?"

"Yes."

"Okay." She raises her palms. "Let's just stay calm. Is your front door locked?"

I nod.

"Did he try to come in?"

"No. He's parked on the street. He was just…." My pulse is racing too fast to think straight. "Just standing by his car, staring at me. We need to call the police."

"Okay." She follows me back to the living room where I've left my phone.

I pluck it off the couch while Becca pushes the curtain aside and peers out the window.

"I don't see anyone."

"What?" I lower my phone. "He's right out front." Exasperated, I move beside Becca, ready to point out the obvious.

"There's no one there," she adds.

17

She's right. I stare out the glass. The street is empty. He's gone.

"He must've left." I exhale. "I still think we should call the police." I back away from the window and lift my phone.

"Wait." Becca puts a hand on my wrist. "There will be a record of a police report, right? We can't prove anyone was out front. What if Steven uses it to try to pin you as…unstable again?"

It would be the sort of thing Steven would use against me. But I'm not about to jeopardize Olivia's safety over fear of what he'll do. "I'm not unstable. I'm worried about Olivia. What if this guy tries to hurt her?"

"I know, but I'm just saying…you should think about how it could look when Steven is hell bent on taking your custody away again."

I chew the inside of my lip. "One of the neighbors might've seen him too."

Becca looks skeptical. "It's dark and almost ten o'clock at night. Could you even see his face?"

I stiffen. "No, not clearly. But it was him. I could tell."

"I believe you." Becca places a reassuring hand on my arm. "But I'm not sure it's worth calling the police tonight. I doubt they can really do anything anyway."

I sink onto the couch. Becca is probably right. Evan's gone, and I don't even know his last name. If I *do* file a police report, Steven will find it. Use it to say my poor choices are endangering our daughter. Again.

I stare at the door to Olivia's room. I can't lose her again.

Becca sits next to me. "How about I stay over tonight? Just in case. Jeff has already put the boys to bed anyway. Then, if this guy shows up again tonight, we call the police. Or, if he keeps stalking you, you get a restraining order."

I nod, suddenly exhausted. "Okay, thank you."

Becca twists toward me, resting her elbow on the back of the couch. "He's probably just trying to get a reaction from you. Weirdos like him feed on attention."

I set my phone on the couch. Hopefully, Becca is right.

CHAPTER FOUR

Four Nights Later

Rob turns to me from the passenger seat of the crew van, his gray hair illuminated by the city lights flickering through the rain-streaked windows as we wind away from the airport toward the harbor. "Great landing tonight."

Behind me, Becca is sandwiched between Nova and Tony, the two other flight attendants on our trip. Tony makes a joke I can't hear, and Becca laughs.

"That was the worst tail wind I've seen in a long time," Rob adds. "But you handled it great."

The captain's words sink deeper than they should. I needed to hear that. "Thank you," I tell him. Even though my leave of absence had nothing to do with my skills as a pilot, I still feel the need to prove myself.

The van pulls to a stop outside our hotel, the harbor air damp and cool against my face. After we unload and drag our roller bags into the lobby, I fall in line behind Becca to check in.

"You ready to go out tonight?" There's a gleam of excitement in Becca's wide-set hazel eyes. "We're heading to The Exchange and someplace called The Green Door, which according to Google is the best place in Boston to pick up hot, single men." She gestures to the two flight attendants in front of us, who are both watching some stupid viral video on one of their phones and giggling. "Tony and Nova are coming too."

"Oh…" I rack my brain for an excuse not to go.

Becca puts a hand on her hip. "Don't tell me you forgot."

I did, actually. Even though I haven't seen Evan since the night Becca slept over, I've been consumed with either trying to make the most of my time with Olivia or worrying Evan might show up again. Bar hopping wasn't on my mind at all.

As the line moves, I wearily drag my suitcase a few inches forward. "Sorry, Bec. I'm going to have to pass. I'm beat. I've hardly slept the last few nights, afraid Evan might come back." I glance at the clock on the wall behind the counter. Our flight from Seattle was delayed two hours, and it's already after ten on Boston time. "And I need to make sure I'm rested for our flights tomorrow."

Plus, the last thing I need right now is to meet some other weirdo who follows me home. Subconsciously, I look over my shoulder, half-expecting Evan to be lurking in the lobby. But there's no one in the lobby but us and the two people working the check-in counter.

"What are you looking at?" Becca asks.

I face forward, chiding myself for being paranoid. "Nothing." *Of course, he's not here. I'm on the other side of the country.*

"You do seem a little tense," Becca says, her expression flickering with concern. "You okay?"

I take a breath and let my posture soften. "Yeah, just tired." I can't afford to appear jumpy to the rest of the crew. I've just returned to work after a mental breakdown and court-ordered rehab.

Holding his room key, Rob waves at us. "See you all in the morning," he says before heading toward the elevators.

"Night, Rob," I say before turning back to Becca.

Becca glances across the lobby at the crowded hotel bar. "We could just grab beers over there if you want. I know you're not drinking, but Tony and Nova are a lot of fun. It could help take your mind off things. Plus..." Becca peers behind me. "I see some cute guys over by the window."

I shake my head as we move to the front of the line. "I can't. But you go and have fun. Have a drink for me."

"Can I help who's next?" a man asks behind the check-in counter.

After Becca steps forward and hands the man her driver's license, she looks over her shoulder at me. "Okay, I get it. But I'm taking a raincheck. Don't think you're getting off the hook that easy."

"Deal," I say as the man behind the desk gives Becca her room key.

At the end of the counter, Nova turns to Tony and nudges him, tilting the screen of her cell phone so he can see. "Have you seen the TikTok with the guy lip-syncing in his car and the airbag goes off mid-song?"

Tony's eyes widen, and he shakes his head. He leans over Nova's shoulder and watches the video playing on her phone until his mouth opens in shock. His broad shoulders cave forward as he nearly chokes on his gum.

"Crazy, right?" Nova drops her phone to her side and turns to Becca. "You two ready to go out?"

"Just me." Becca steps aside for me to check in. "Claire's taking a raincheck."

A pang catches me as I take in the three of them, light-hearted and ready for a night I can't join. Part of me longs to be in that place too, able to let go and just have fun. "Go ahead," I tell her. "Don't wait for me. And have fun tonight."

"I will, and you get some rest. If I meet any hot, single guys, I'll be sure to get their numbers for you." Becca winks.

I frown. "Please don't."

"No promises." She grins before turning toward the other flight attendants, dragging her roller bag behind her.

"Okay, guys. Let's hurry and change," she says to Nova and Tony as the front desk manager returns my ID.

"Would you like two keys or one?" he asks.

"One is fine, thanks."

My stomach grumbles when I start toward the elevators. I swing into the convenience kiosk in the corner of the lobby and buy a bag of pretzels before heading up to my room. I'm alone when I step into the elevator, exhaustion creeping over me now that I don't have to put on an "I'm fine" act for the others. After double checking my room number, I press the button for the tenth floor.

Waiting for the doors to close, I check my watch and let out a sigh. It's too late to call and say goodnight to Olivia. A man steps in front of the elevator doors as they start to close. My jaw drops, and my room key slips from my fingers as he flashes me a menacing smile, revealing perfectly straight, white teeth.

"Hello, Claire."

CHAPTER FIVE

STEP BACK, BUMPING into the handrail, as Evan squeezes inside the elevator right before the doors close. I open my mouth to scream. But what good would it do? We're already ascending. I close my white-knuckled grip around the handrail and scoot as far away from Evan as I can in the tight, enclosed space.

How the hell did he find me at my hotel? Was he on my flight? No, I would've seen him getting off.

"What are you doing here?"

He casually presses the button for the eighth floor, then clasps his hands behind his back. "Going to my room of course."

With a smirk, he leans against the elevator wall, clearly enjoying watching me squirm. He's wearing similar clothes to what he wore on our date, jeans and a fitted polo shirt.

"That's not what I meant," I say through clenched teeth. "What do you want?"

He cocks his head toward me. As he returns my stare, there's a glint of darkness in his deep blue eyes. It's so unmistakable that I wonder how I could've been so easily charmed by him, even though it was short lived.

The elevator stops on the fifth floor. I make a move to get out when a gray-haired woman steps inside, making me pause. Evan knows this isn't my floor. What if he follows me out?

I scoot back against the wall, feeling safer with the woman between us. Not that this petite woman could defend me against Evan's bulk, but I doubt he's going to try to assault me in front of a witness.

The elevator stops on the eighth floor, and when Evan steps out, I heave a sigh of relief. Before the doors close, he throws me a look over his shoulder.

"Goodnight, Claire."

When the elevator lifts toward my floor, I shut my eyes and lean my head against the mirrored wall.

"Are you all right, dear?"

I open my eyes to find the woman studying me, her expression inquisitive but kind. Spotting my reflection in the elevator's mirrored wall, I notice my pilot's uniform looks at odds with the panic in my eyes. I force my face into something steadier, more confident. "Fine, thanks." I lie. "It's just been a long day."

By the time I step off onto my floor, the elevator feels like it's closing in on me. I look around to make sure I'm alone before I hurry to my room. My fingers tremble as I lock the dead bolt and chain behind me.

I press my palm against the door and drop my gaze to the floor. *Who the hell is this guy? And what does he want with me?*

"And you don't know his last name?" The young night-shift officer taking my report looks up from his laptop to meet my gaze across the table. It's pushed against the wall in the small, windowless room, and cold air blows from a vent in the ceiling. The hum of the fluorescent light fills the silence between us.

"Well, no. The dating app doesn't show last names." Given the officer's age, I would think he should know this.

"You have any photos of him?"

I shake my head. "When I got back on the app, his profile had been deleted."

He sits back in his seat and folds his arms, a flicker of annoyance on his face. Apparently, I'm wasting his time.

"Do you have his phone number?"

"I did." I bring a hand to my face, recalling the moment I hastily deleted our text thread. I'd just gotten home from our date, and seeing his text, *goodnight,* creeped me out. "But I deleted our texts. So now I don't have it."

The look on the officer's face makes me cringe. "I didn't know I was going to need it," I add as if my action needs justification. "Wait." I sit up straight. "I can get his number from my cell phone provider, right? Since we texted?"

"Yeah." He nods, stifling a yawn. "You should be able to." The officer types something into his laptop.

I lean back in my seat. At least that's *something.*

"And when you saw him tonight," the officer keeps his fingers on the keyboard, "did he hurt you?"

"No."

"Threaten you?"

I shake my head. "But he's *stalking* me. And he has an anger problem—I saw it on our first date. He's dangerous.

I'm sure of it." I sit forward. "And now he's followed me *across the country.*"

My breath quickens, as if the room is running out of air. The cop looks unmoved. I get that he's probably seen his share of crazy in this job, but how is he not getting the seriousness of this?

"And you're sure it was the same guy?"

I lean forward, not bothering to hide my irritation. "*Yes. This guy is unhinged.*" I press my palm flat on the table. "Unstable. He said my name tonight before the elevator doors closed, and he had this..." I close my eyes, trying to think of how to describe it. "Crazy look in his eye. Like he was coming for me."

The officer stares at his computer screen. "Based on what you've told me, there's nothing we can do. He hasn't broken any laws."

My lungs stiffen. "He's probably still at my hotel, waiting for me to get back. Can't you at least bring him in for questioning?"

The officer looks up from his screen. "For being in a hotel lobby? No. It's a public place. He might even be a guest at the hotel."

"Because he's stalking me!" My shout fills the tiny room. "He's probably on the hotel security footage." My pulse spikes. "Can't you run facial recognition on it to figure out who he is?"

He sighs as if I'm a child asking too many questions rather than a woman in danger.

"We would need a search warrant to get the hotel security footage. And no judge is going to sign off on one without just cause."

"But he—"

The officer lifts a palm in the air. "Which we don't have. Look, I'll take down your details and write a report. That way it will be on record if anything else happens."

"Like he kills me?"

The officer frowns. "My recommendation is to file a restraining order once you find his phone number, which we can use to get his full name and, hopefully, his address. You said you're from Seattle. How long are you in town for?"

"I leave tomorrow. I'm an airline pilot. Here on a layover."

"Then I suggest waiting to file the restraining order until you get home. Until we know who this guy is, we can't serve him—and without service, a restraining order can't be enforced. Once you're back in Washington and have his name or a way to identify him, you should file there. Let me just double check your contact information before you go."

I slump forward, resting my elbows on the desk as he checks the spelling of my name and address. At least I should be able to get a restraining order when I get home to keep him from coming around, especially when I have Olivia.

The officer's expression darkens while he stares at his screen. "It says here you were ordered into treatment after a DUI in Washington a few months back?"

I gape at him when he meets my gaze. *Was he running a background check on me?* "What does that have to do with anything?"

"That didn't affect your job as an airline pilot?"

I study him in stunned silence. Is he feeding his own curiosity now, or something else? "No. I had prescribed pills in my system, and I've never taken them at work." I stop myself before adding that I don't remember taking those pills in the first place. That I would never endanger my daughter on purpose. Because none of this is his business. "So, I was allowed to return to work after completing a treatment program." I lean forward, pressing my ribs against the table. "I'm sorry, what does this have to do with my having a stalker?"

The officer rubs the stubble on the bottom of his chin. "Have you had anything to drink tonight?"

I stand. "This is unbelievable. No. Again, what does that have to do with anything?"

He closes his laptop with a deep breath, his shoulders stiffening. His gaze lingers on me, cautious, as if bracing to calm down an unruly prisoner. "Get some rest. And make sure to have a safe flight tomorrow."

I narrow my eyes. *What's that supposed to mean? Is he insinuating I might have a drink before flying a plane full of people?* I swallow. *Like I took the Clonazepam before driving Olivia that night.* I push the thought away and give him one last look before opening the door and marching toward the exit. From inside another room, a woman's heaving sobs reverberate into the hallway.

When I step outside, the air is damp from the light mist falling. I dig a hand into my purse for my phone to order an Uber and nearly run into a female officer who's about to enter the building.

"Excuse me." She continues past me.

"Sorry," I mumble, blinking back tears.

As I wait for my ride, I contemplate calling Becca to tell her everything that's happened. My hands tremble with anger over the officer questioning my sobriety rather than taking me seriously. But it's already after midnight, and if I want any sleep tonight, I need to try to put the night's events out of my mind. Talking about it will likely only rile me up more. Thunderstorms are predicted tomorrow, and I need to be rested for whatever challenges that might bring.

When the Uber arrives, I climb into the back, my body heavy as the weight of the day hits me all at once. Staring out the window on the drive back to the hotel, I can't help but think that Becca was right. Going to the police was completely pointless.

CHAPTER SIX

RAIN BEATS AGAINST the flight deck windscreen.
"We were supposed to be getting a jump seater.
Probably a Vantage Skies pilot since this is one of their hubs." Beside me, Rob checks his watch, the glow from the instruments sharpening the lines of his face. "But looks like they might be a no-show."

I hold back a yawn and open the pre-flight checklist card. After returning to my hotel room from the police station, I'd lain awake in the dark, seeing Evan's creepy smile every time I closed my eyes. Not only was I infuriated by the adolescent officer questioning my sobriety, but my mind whirled with how Evan could've tracked me to my Boston hotel. The last time I looked at the clock it was after four in the morning.

I rub my eyes the same way Olivia does when she's tired, and my mind shifts to her, already at school. The thought of picking her up tonight lightens my mood. Soon, I'll be 30,000 feet in the air, where Evan can't get to me, and then I'll be home. And I'll get a restraining order.

Becca pops her head through the flight deck door. "You

two need anything before takeoff? Coffee?" she asks as if reading my mind.

"I'll take a coffee. Thanks, Bec."

"Me too," Rob says.

"You got it." She turns for the first-class galley, her sleek ponytail swaying behind her. She's wearing less makeup than usual, but aside from that and her bloodshot eyes from her night out, Becca looks her typical sophisticated self.

I still haven't told her about seeing Evan last night. I called her this morning, but she didn't pick up. When she climbed into the crew van beside me, she explained she forgot to set an alarm and woke up half an hour before we were due to leave the hotel. I was dying to tell her the whole ride to the airport but didn't want the rest of the crew to hear.

"Looks like it's going to be one of those days in Denver, with convective activity and low-level wind shears forecasted," Rob says. "Are you comfortable taking this leg? If not, you can take the next leg to make it even."

"I'll take this leg," I say without hesitation—eager to show I can handle it, as much for myself as for the captain. I move down the checklist when I hear the thump of the forward entry door closing. I reach for the PA microphone. "Flight attendants, please prepare the cabin for departure and crosscheck."

The shuffle of footsteps fills the flight deck as I replace the PA mic on its holder. The click of the jump seat harness follows after someone drops into place.

"Hey, I'm Mitch. Thanks for letting me hitch a ride with you guys," a man says from directly behind me.

It must be our jump seater, I think, annoyed that he didn't have the courtesy to wait to introduce himself until we had finished our preflight checklist. A waft of the jump seater's cologne assaults my nostrils. I get a sense of déjà vu, but I can't place it.

Rob twists in his seat. "Oh, hi. I'm Rob. Wasn't sure if you were going to make it."

"Here you go." Becca appears and hands Rob and me our coffees.

"Thanks," I tell her.

"Looks like it's going to be a bumpy ride home," Rob says after taking his coffee.

Becca groans. "Oh, great. Just what I need, with a full first-class breakfast service."

Normally, I'd share Becca's sentiment about the weather—storms mean added stress on the flight deck, and after being placed on leave pending my completion of rehab, I can't afford any mistakes. But today, I'll take the business that comes along with the stress of battling the storm. Anything to take my mind off Evan.

"Can I get you anything to drink before pushback?" I hear Becca ask the jump seat pilot seated behind me.

"No, thanks. I'm good."

Nova's voice comes over our intercom. "Aft cabin secure."

Becca steps out of the flight deck, closing the door behind her as I announce, "Before start checklist complete," and stow the checklist in its slot on the glareshield.

I hear a couple of thumps against the side of the airplane and look down to see the ground crewman signaling with his hands that he wants to remove the ground power cord. I lift my gaze, seeing that the APU is powering the airplane. I give a thumbs up to the ground crewman and key the microphone.

"Boston Ground Cascadia three two three, gate C36,

ready to pushback with Sierra," I say as the young officer's words from last night gnaw at the forefront of my thoughts, the skepticism written on his face seared in my memory. *And you're sure it was the same guy?*

The possibility that I could've imagined seeing Evan last night fills me with even more terror than him following me across the country. I glance at the pre-flight checklist, forcing away the thought that I might've missed something. I didn't. I know what I'm doing.

Steven's face flashes in my mind, along with his disgusted look of condescension after I forgot to pick up Olivia from school right after I moved out. His voice echoes in my head, dripping with contempt.

"How could you have forgotten? She's your only child."

"This wasn't my day," I said, confused by his adamance that it was my fault Olivia had no one to pick her up.

Steven held up his phone. "I emailed you three days ago asking you to pick her up for me today." He scrolled down, keeping the screen facing me. "And you replied, saying you would."

I stepped forward to read the words I had no memory of typing. Then I remembered. I'd been home alone Monday night and consumed a whole bottle of wine to fill the void of Olivia not being home with me, which I wasn't about to tell Steven.

"Well?" His ice blue eyes pierced through mine like a knife.

"I—I guess I forgot. I'm sorry."

"Claire." Rob saying my name through the headset pulls me back to the present. "This is Mitch, our jump seater."

I turn in my seat, pulling one of the headphones behind my ear. "Nice to—"

My throat closes around my breath as I take in the man seated directly behind me wearing a Vantage Skies pilot's uniform. The name on his flight crew ID lanyard says Mitchell Ortiz, which must be his real name. Now I know why his cologne—the distinctive mix of pine trees and citrus—was familiar.

He smiles at my shock. The same smile he flashed me last night outside the elevator. The same smile he gave me at Olivia's school, and at the end of our terrible date.

"Nice to meet you, Claire. Thanks for letting me bum a ride."

CHAPTER SEVEN

R OB RELEASES THE parking brake and tells the tug driver we're cleared for pushback. I spin around to face forward, my pulse pounding in my ears. My mind reels. What the hell is he doing here?

A voice crackles through my headset as Rob rounds the corner at the end of the taxiway and approaches the runway hold line. "Cascadia three two three, the wind is two four zero at eight, runway two two left cleared for takeoff."

Is he impersonating a pilot? No, he couldn't do that. He had to go through a fingerprint scanner to get through security. Unless he bought a passenger ticket and changed into a stolen pilot uniform after going through security.

"Cascadia three two three, without delay, cleared for takeoff runway two two left," the tower repeats with an anxious tone.

"Roger, Cascadia three two three. Cleared for takeoff two two left," Rob replies when I don't respond to the control tower.

He cocks his head toward me as I sit frozen, making no

move for the controls, momentarily paralyzed at the thought of being trapped on the flight deck with my stalker for the next five hours. "Claire? You okay?"

I clear my throat. "Yes, fine," I manage.

Rob shoves the thrust levers forward and turns onto the runway. "We better move before the tower cancels our takeoff clearance."

I'm racking my brain for an excuse to abort the takeoff. But what can I say? If I cause a high-speed abort because I'm afraid of the pilot seated behind me, I can imagine the news headline. *PILOT ABORTS TAKEOFF, ACCUSES JUMP SEATER OF STALKING.*

No, I could lose my job. Worse than that, Steven would use it to claim I'm unstable and regain full custody of Olivia.

Rob keeps the airplane rolling. After lining up on the centerline, he says, "Your airplane."

I could say that I'm sick—a sudden, debilitating headache. But even that could make the news. Steven's last words to me ring in my ears. *One slip up, just one, and I'll make sure Olivia comes back to live with me full time. For good.*

"My airplane." I push the thrust levers up. When the engines stabilize, I press the TOGA button on the front of the levers. "Set takeoff power."

I keep moving the thrust levers forward to the takeoff setting. As Rob checks the power setting, I force myself to take a deep breath.

"Power set, airspeed's alive. There's 80 knots looking for 137," he says.

"That checks." I sit calmly as though nothing is wrong, knowing I have no choice. I can't give Steven any more ammo to use against me. Plus, it's not like I'm alone with this creep. Rob is here.

I subconsciously hold slight forward pressure on the control yoke and steer the airplane down the centerline with the rudder pedals. As the G-force from our acceleration pulls me against my seatback, I try to convince myself that everything is going to be fine. It's only five hours.

What's the worst that can happen?

When we reach our cruising altitude, Rob lifts the PA microphone. "Ladies and gentlemen, this is Rob from the flight deck. We've reached our cruising altitude, and you're free to move about the cabin. But we ask that you keep your seatbelts fastened while in your seats, as we're expecting a bit of a bumpy ride today as we make our way to Denver. Thank you for flying with us, and we wish you a pleasant flight."

A terrifying thought rips through my mind as Evan-slash-Mitch makes small talk with Rob through our headsets about last night's Seahawks game. *What if this guy has a gun?* It's possible, I realize, if he went through the Known Crewmember security checkpoint and bypassed security.

"What about you, Claire? Did you see last night's game?"

Hearing "Mitch" say my name through my headset makes me nearly jump out of my seat.

Rob must've noticed, because when I meet his gaze, he's eyeing me strangely.

Stop letting him get to you. You have to relax. Maybe Becca is right about weirdos like him feeding on attention. If so, I'm not giving him the satisfaction of a reaction. "Uh, no. I… went straight to bed."

"That's a shame." Mitch breathes into his mouthpiece. "You missed a hell of a game."

"You sure you're okay?" Rob asks me. "You look pale."

"Yeah, I'm good." I unbuckle my shoulder straps. "Really," I add, but the captain looks unconvinced. "I just need to finish my coffee." I reach for my cup. "The time change on these cross-country trips always gets me."

Mitch goes back to talking to Rob about the two-point conversion that won the game, and my thoughts return to how he could be here, in the jump seat. He said he worked in graphic design. A lie, obviously, along with his name.

Maybe he's married. That could explain why he used a fake name and deleted his account on the app. The momentary comfort I get from this possibility evaporates as it strikes me that him being a philanderer still doesn't explain everything. If he lied about his job and really is a pilot for Vantage Skies, that explains him being here and at my hotel, but it doesn't explain him showing up at Olivia's school or my house.

I unbuckle my seatbelt and turn to Rob. "I'm gonna use the lav." I pull off my headphones, aware of Mitch's eyes on me as I climb out of my seat. If he weren't here, I would have to call Becca to stay in the flight deck while I used the bathroom—FAA rules mean we always have to have two authorized crewmembers in the flight deck. Fortunately, jump seat pilots count, because I need to talk to her—alone. I meet Mitch's gaze momentarily before looking away. The hard look that radiates from his icy blue eyes seems out of place on his stunningly attractive face.

After closing the flight deck door behind me, I spot Becca bringing one of the first-class passengers a bottle of water. I move past the lavatory and wait for her in the galley.

Becca comes around the corner carrying an empty beer can. "Oh!" She places a hand over her heart. "You scared me. I saw you come out, but I thought you were using the lavatory." Seeing my expression, she turns serious. "What's wrong?"

"It's *the guy.* It's why I called you this morning. He was staying at our hotel and got in the elevator with me last night."

"*What?*"

"I went to the police, but like you said, there wasn't anything they could do."

"You should've called me!" She steps forward, placing a hand on my arm. "I would've come with you."

"Becca, he's here. In the jump seat."

Her face contorts in confusion. "What? Mitch? No." She steps back. "Are you messing with me?"

I shake my head. "Of course, not! *I'm freaking out.*"

She casts a guarded look over her shoulder. "Shh. The passengers might hear you."

I put my hands on my hips and attempt to suck in a steadying breath.

"But your date wasn't a pilot, right? Didn't he tell you he worked in graphic design?"

I throw up my hands. "He must've lied."

Becca crosses her arms, tapping her fingers against her elbow. "Has he said anything to you? On the flight deck?"

"Not much. He's acting like we've never met before."

Becca's perfectly groomed eyebrows knit together. "I've flown with Mitch before. He was in the jump seat on my flight back from Tampa a few months ago. Are you're sure it's the same guy?"

"Yes!" I press my fingertips against my temples. "I'm telling you, it's *the guy.*"

Becca shoots me a sharp look and puts a finger to her lips. "You have got to keep your voice down," she says, lowering her voice to a whisper, gesturing to the cabin behind her. "They can hear you."

I nod, knowing she's right. I turn and pace the tiny space. We go over a bump, rattling the drink cans inside the galley cupboards.

"Are you still taking your antidepressants?"

I stop and face Becca, my mouth agape. "What does that have to do with anything?" It strikes me that I forgot to take it yesterday, and this morning, with everything that's happened in the last twenty-four hours. But so what?

"I just read an article about a woman who suddenly stopped her antidepressants—days later, police found her walking along a highway confused and disoriented. It said if you stop taking them cold turkey, it can cause short-term memory lapses, even delusions."

"I'm not having delusions!"

"Is everything okay?" Behind Becca stands one of the first-class passengers, a middle-aged man wearing a look of concern.

Becca whirls around, flashing the man smile. "Yes, everything's fine. Just having a little girl talk. Can I get you anything?"

The man eyes me warily, fiddling with a button on his shirt nervously before responding. "I'll take another gin and tonic."

"You got it," Becca says, closing the galley curtain after the man retreats to his seat. She whirls around to face me.

I lower my voice. "I'm not losing it, Becca."

She presses her matte-red-lipsticked lips together. "I'm

not saying you are. Look, if you think it's the guy, I believe you. It just seems…odd, like too much of a coincidence for him to be a pilot and be here on our flight."

I press a palm against the metal galley cupboard. "I know. That's why it scares me."

Becca reaches in front of me and pulls a mini bottle of gin from the cupboard. "Maybe you should talk to your therapist about this when we get home."

I stand still, watching Becca retrieve a can of tonic water from a pull-out drawer. "You think this is all in my head. Don't you?"

"I just think you've been through a lot this past year." She squeezes my forearm.

I resist the urge to recoil from her touch, knowing what she's insinuating. That I'm crazy. Losing my mind.

Her expression softens. "All I'm saying is it might be good to check in with your therapist, get her take on all this."

I blink back the tears that spring to my eyes, my best friend's doubt hitting me like a punch to the gut. "I should get back." I slide past her without another word.

I type the code into a panel on the wall and wait for Rob to unlock the door to the flight deck. After I step inside, Mitch offers me a pleasant smile over the top of his aviation magazine, making my blood run cold.

The plane dips, and my stomach drops as the floor moves beneath my feet. I press my hand against the wall to keep from ending up in Mitch's lap. I avoid his gaze, feeling his eyes on me as I climb into my seat before we hit another bump.

It's him. Isn't it? Could my mind really be playing tricks on me?

I pull on my headset, and Rob turns to me, his voice coming through the headphones.

"Looks like that thunderstorm is moving south, so we likely won't need to divert. We're still going to have a strong crosswind though when we land in Denver."

"I had a trip to Tampa last month," Mitch chimes in. "Worst crosswind I've ever had. We probably should have diverted. I was worried we were going to roll off the runway."

Rob starts telling us about the time he was struck by lightning on a flight to Dallas, but all I can do is mentally replay what Becca said about my memory problems. My thoughts drift back to the night of the accident.

Is it possible that I'm mistaking Mitch for my bad date? That I'm unraveling all over again?

CHAPTER EIGHT

Six Months Earlier

WHEN I GOT to my old house to pick up Olivia, I was surprised when Steven asked me to come inside. Things had been particularly contentious between us these last few weeks since we'd separated; we were barely on speaking terms. Steven's adolescent girlfriend was at work, so it was just the three of us. After Olivia took me upstairs by the hand to show me her new overpriced dollhouse—their latest attempt to buy her love—Steven came up and told Olivia to stay in her room while Mommy and Daddy talked privately.

When we got to the kitchen, I sat on a barstool I'd picked out last year at Restoration Hardware.

He set a mug in front of me. "I made your favorite tea."

As I inhaled the vanilla almond scent steaming up from the mug, I wondered if Steven was about to apologize for his affair, maybe even ask me if I wanted to reconcile. Steven stood on the other side of the island, leaning against the cabinets with his arms folded like I'd seen him do a million times before. I racked my brain for a response. Until that moment, I hadn't considered getting back together a possibility.

He'd been a complete jerk to me ever since we'd separated, but some of that was my fault. I *had* forgotten to pick up Olivia at school, and I'd missed our initial court hearing to settle our temporary custody agreement. I still didn't know how I'd missed the email from my attorney—aside from being an emotional wreck those last few weeks.

When Steven had told me he was seeing a nurse at work and wanted a divorce, my world had flipped upside down. Even though we'd been having problems, and I was convinced his stature as a surgeon had added to his superiority complex, it had still shocked me.

"Well, what do you want to talk about?" I took a sip from my tea, noting he'd even remembered to sweeten it with agave.

He nodded toward my mug. "Did I make it how you like it?"

"You did." I took another drink, swallowing hard against the surge of emotion, hating that I still felt anything for him after his betrayal.

Holding my mug with both hands, I watched his chest rise as he appeared to steel himself for what he was about to tell me. It struck me that I may have read this situation all wrong. What if his girlfriend was pregnant? I'd had a tubal after Olivia was born. Since then, we'd never had to worry about birth control. I drank more of my tea, which was no longer comforting, and braced myself for whatever Steven was about to say.

He unfolded his arms and placed the heels of his hands on the granite countertop behind him. "Since we separated, your behavior has been not only unreliable, but frankly…unstable. I have grave concerns over how this is affecting Olivia. Actually, I had these concerns before our separation, which was part of the reason I wanted a divorce."

I set my mug on the counter with a *clang* as tea sloshed over the side. "Is this about the court hearing? That was a mix-up. My attorney's office said they emailed me about it, but I never received it."

"It's more than the court date, and you know it."

His familiar look of condescension sent a spark of anger through me. I glared at him in disgusted awe that he could be so unfeeling about ripping our family apart. Our separation hadn't affected his functionality in the least. I had to call out sick for a trip because I didn't feel safe to fly in my emotionally wrought state, while Steven had gone on with his life and career as though nothing had happened.

I was done walking on eggshells around him like I had when we were married. "Oh, stop." He was trying to shame me for forgetting to pick up Olivia at school for him last week—which I already apologized for. "What's your point, Steven?"

"From now on, I'll be pursuing full custody of Olivia through my attorney. I didn't have to warn you, but I thought it was only fair that you know."

My jaw fell open. "Full custody? Have you lost your freaking mind? I'm her mother, Steven. She needs me. I need her." I stood from the barstool and moved around the island, refusing to let him get away with this. I jabbed a pointer finger toward his chest, shaking with rage. "I'm not about to let you take Olivia away from me and claim I'm some kind of unfit parent. The courts will see through your lies."

He sighed, eyeing me as if I were the unreasonable one.

"You can waste your money if you want," I added. "But I'll die before I let you take my child from me."

He frowned. "You've been overmedicating yourself for your anxiety, Claire. It's a safety concern."

I scoffed at his attempt to gaslight me. "I'm not *over medicating.*" I'd recently been placed on some anxiety meds, yes, but at a low dose to help me deal with the upheaval of the divorce.

Steven flicked his gaze toward Olivia's upstairs room as if to make sure my raised voice hadn't disturbed her.

"I shouldn't have said anything." Steven lifted his hands in the air, backing away from me. "I knew you'd overreact." He shook his head. "I don't want you upsetting Olivia any more than your behavior already has."

I gaped at him, at a loss for how I could've ever married such a monster. *"Overreact?* Do you hear yourself? You're talking about taking *my child* away from me."

He motioned to my mug on the counter, his expression void of emotion. "Why don't you calm down and finish your tea. I'll play with Olivia until you're in a better mental state to take her home. Or, if not, she can stay here with me."

Despite the rage whirling inside me like a tornado, I said nothing as I watched Steven make for the stairs, knowing there was nothing I could say that he wouldn't try to use against me. Tears sprung to my eyes. As much as I hated that I'd let him get to me, I sunk back onto the barstool and took a deep breath, not wanting Olivia to see me upset.

Upstairs, I heard Steven let out an animal roar and Olivia respond with a cackle. Hearing him go on as if nothing had happened only infuriated me more. My hand trembled as I reached for my tea.

Steven didn't care what was best for Olivia. This was all about protecting his reputation. It wasn't a great look to leave your family for a twenty-year-old. He was trying to gain sympathy and turn himself into a victim by making me look like a lunatic.

I finished my tea in the quiet kitchen, and a strong sense of calm came over me. As I got up and moved toward the stairs, my anger was replaced by resolve. Steven had no grounds to say I was an unfit parent.

I placed a hand on the banister and called upstairs. "Olivia, sweetie? It's time to go. Say goodbye to daddy."

Seeing her bound to the top of the steps, her blonde hair in a ponytail that matched the doll she clutched at her chest, filled my heart with warmth. Over my dead body would he ever take her from me.

CHAPTER NINE

THE FLIGHT DECK rattles as we hit a pocket of rough air. I lean into the control column, my hands ready to hold the wings level if the autopilot can't keep up, as the turbulence shoves us sideways.

Rob unbuckles his seatbelt. "My coffee's kicking in," he says into his mic. "I better hit the lav before this turbulence gets worse."

He takes off his headphones as I rack my brain for a reason to tell him he can't leave me alone with this psychopath. But what would I say? Rob climbs out of his seat while I keep my hand on the control column and try to dispel the wild scenarios that run through my head. What will Mitch do once we're alone?

When the flight deck door closes behind Rob, my lungs cinch with panic. I should've stopped him. What if Mitch attacks me? Tries to take down the plane?

A male voice crackles over the radio. "Cascadia three two three, contact Chicago Center on one two five point two."

"Cascadia three two three, roger," I respond, setting the frequency in the standby window of the Com 1 radio.

"Chicago on one two five two."

After checking in with Chicago Center, I gaze out the windshield, watching a puffy layer of clouds roll beneath the nose. Mitch, or whatever his real name is, remains silent behind me. With Rob gone, now is my chance to confront him. I whirl around to demand to know what the hell he's doing here on my flight. And Olivia's school. My house. Making a fake dating profile and lying about his identity.

Mitch looks up from his aviation magazine, and I study his face. The menacing glint in his eyes I'd seen earlier has been replaced with what seems to be curiosity.

We hit another patch of rough air. I face forward as the nose lifts toward the sky. I glance at the instruments while the autopilot corrects, and the airplane stabilizes.

Becca's words fly through my head as I depress the mic button to demand to know what Mitch is doing here and why he's been stalking me. *You've been through a lot this past year.* Her way of saying I'm having some sort of delusion, rather than a stalker.

According to my therapist, the trauma of nearly losing Olivia twice—first to the car accident and then to Steven—caused my mental breakdown. My uncontrollable hysteria in the courtroom caused me to be admitted to the psych ward, and after that, I refused to eat or speak for days. The trauma was also likely the reason I don't remember taking the Clonazepam before driving Olivia that night. It was my subconscious way of dealing with the guilt in the aftermath of what I'd done.

What if Becca is right? I lift my finger off the mic.

"Claire, tell me."

I stiffen at Mitch's smooth voice coming through my headset.

"What do you think Olivia is doing right now? You must miss her so much when you're away from her."

The flight deck seems to drop in temperature, and a chill settles over my skin. I'm not crazy. He really is the guy from my bad date, who's been stalking me ever since.

"I wonder who will be picking Olivia up from school today. Steven, or his college-age girlfriend."

Hearing my daughter's name on his lips for a second time sends a surge of anger through my limbs. I spin in my seat. "What the hell do you want with me?"

Mitch grins in response. Instinctively, I glance around the cockpit to find something to protect myself. But nothing looks lethal enough. The crash axe is mounted behind Rob's seat, but I can't imagine using it. The flight deck phone rings. Heart pounding, I twist to pick up the phone without taking my eyes off my stalker.

"This is Claire," I say, still facing Mitch.

"Claire," Becca gasps. "There's an emergency. It's Rob." She speaks fast, her tone clipped with panic. "He collapsed when he came out of the lav. He—" her voice breaks. "He was foaming at the mouth. Oh, God. I think he had a seizure. He stopped breathing, and we can't find a pulse." She breathes into the line. "Two passengers are giving him CPR, but we need to get on the ground. *Now.*"

My gaze snaps to the nav screen to find the closest airport. It looks like Peoria, which is nearly forty minutes away. "Make an announcement," I tell her as turbulence rattles the control panel. "Ask if there's a doctor, nurse, or medic on board. But don't say it's for the captain; we don't want to induce panic among the passengers." Although it's not like they can keep that a secret. If Rob collapsed at the front of first class, word has likely already spread. "I'll declare an emergency."

My hand shakes while I cradle the flight deck phone and get on the radio, aware of my stalker sitting in silence behind me. I sit sideways, keeping Mitch in my periphery. "Center, Cascadia three two three, we've got a medical emergency onboard, and we need to divert to Peoria."

"Cascadia three two three, roger, descend and maintain flight level one eight zero and cleared direct to Peoria."

"Anything I can do to help?" Mitch asks.

He stares me down. We both know that in a situation like this, when the captain has been incapacitated, the jump seat pilot is usually expected to take their seat. But I don't want Mitch anywhere near me, let alone sitting right next to me— in reach of all the controls.

"No," I bark. For all I know, he caused this. And he could be planning to kill me next. I need to get him out of the flight deck. "Actually, yes. Go to the main cabin and see if you can help." I work to keep the tremor out of my voice, not liking the idea of Mitch being around the other crew and passengers either, but at least he can't take down the plane from the back.

"You know I can't do that," he says. "Per protocol, we can't open the flight deck door."

I purse my lips together, my heart pounding against my ribs as I stare at his maddeningly relaxed face. Technically, he's right. The flight deck should be on lockdown in case this is an act of terror, a ruse for a hijacker to get access to the flight deck. I shouldn't open the flight deck door for the rest of the flight. My throat tightens. But what if the hijacker is *already in here?*

The shrill ring of the flight deck phone interrupts my thoughts. I jump in my seat before snatching it off my lap. "This is Claire."

"There's a military doctor on board." Becca's voice is breathy. "They've connected Rob to an AED, but still no pulse. They're doing CPR. From Rob's skin color, his seizure, and the smell around Rob's mouth, the doctor thinks he might've been poisoned. He says it could be cyanide—he's seen it before. Overseas."

My heart lurches into my throat as I lock eyes with the man seated behind me. The edges of his mouth lift into a slight smile, causing a ripple of terror to travel down my body. He had to have slipped Rob the poison. My gaze moves to Rob's empty coffee cup in the cup holder of his seat. He could've done it when I went to the lav.

"Claire, I—" Becca breaks into a sob.

My mind races. How long will it be before we're on the ground? "Becca, I need you to stay calm, okay?" I say more to myself than to her.

I cast a look over my shoulder at Mitch, who studies me from his seat, and brace myself for him to attack me and try to take over the controls. Becca said she's flown with him before. *How did this lunatic get hired as an airline pilot?*

Becca's voice wobbles. "The doctor wants to know how long until we land."

"Thirty minutes."

I hear Becca take the phone away from her mouth and call out the time. A pause. "He says that's too long."

"That's how long it takes to get down from this altitude,

maybe a few minutes less. Tell him to keep doing his best for Rob. I'll get us on the ground as soon as possible. I have to go. Need to start our descent."

I drop the handset back in my lap and glance at Mitch, who's made no attempt to move from his seat, before setting 18000 in the altitude window of the MCP and selecting LVL CHG. The thrust levers slowly retard to idle as the nose drops, and the airplane begins a descent. I pull up the speed brake lever to expedite our descent. I peer around the cramped flight deck for something to use to defend myself aside from the crash axe, imagining Mitch's hands clamping around my throat. My gaze glides over the binder beside my seat and the flight deck phone on my lap before landing on the fire extinguisher fastened to the bulkhead behind Rob's seat—which I can reach without getting up.

"You poisoned him, didn't you?" I say, returning my attention to the controls. I get no response. My face flushes with anger. "Why?" Again, no answer. I turn my face sideways, aware of him sitting still in my periphery as I fix my gaze on the fire extinguisher. "What do you want with me?" I shout. Still nothing.

I face forward, shoving the rage down, forcing my focus back to the controls. Getting us on the ground safely is the only choice I have. I take a deep breath and lift the PA microphone.

"Ladies and gentlemen, due to a medical emergency, we will be making a landing at Peoria in just over twenty minutes." I pause, summoning steadiness into my voice despite the fear rising inside me. "I have started our descent and ask that everyone return to their seats with their seatbelts fastened for the remainder of the flight. I apologize for the inconvenience and thank you for your understanding."

After replacing the PA mic, I'm struck by a terrifying thought: If Mitch really is a pilot, he doesn't need to keep me alive to land the plane. But then why hasn't he attacked me already? I whirl around, narrowing my eyes at the man sitting calmly in the jump seat. "I'll ask you again. Why did you do this? What do you want?"

His expression is unreadable, void of emotion. It sickeningly reminds me of Steven.

"I didn't do anything."

"Stop lying! You've been stalking me since our date, *Evan*. And now you're in *my* jump seat, and the captain is dead."

He's calm. Too calm. He doesn't say a word, but the glimmer in his eye says he's *enjoying* this.

"I'm about to call the ground authorities to let them know what's happening. The FBI will be waiting for you once we land," I add, hoping to summon some sort of response out of him. "I don't know who you are or what you want, but you aren't going to get away with this." Not that the FBI will matter if he kills me at 30,000 feet. I think of calling Becca, asking her if there's an off-duty cop on board—that would send her a message that I need help subduing the man behind me.

"I wouldn't do that if I were you, Claire."

"And why not?" I stare at him, unblinking. Daring him to challenge me. "Tell me what the hell is going on."

"If Rob was poisoned," Mitch finally says. "There's only one person on board who could've done it, and it wasn't me. It was Becca, the flight attendant who made his coffee and brought it to him."

I scoff. If 136 lives weren't on the line, I might've laughed. He can't possibly believe I would buy that.

"I couldn't have done anything to it from back here," he adds, seemingly reading the disbelief on my face. "Plus, you were here. You would've seen me."

I go still, not wanting to believe him. "She'd never. She wouldn't." But my voice lacks the certainty it had a moment ago. Now that I think about it, Rob had finished his coffee before I left to use the lav. I study the door to the main cabin, and before I can stop myself, I'm imagining Becca slipping a cyanide capsule out of her blazer and dropping it into Rob's cup. I return my gaze to Mitch, feeling my eyes narrow to a glare. "You could've slipped him something when I left the flight deck. Offered him gum or a mint laced with poison."

He cooly returns my stare. "I didn't." He raises his eyebrows. "You don't believe me? Becca told you she'd flown with me before, didn't she? That I couldn't be the guy you met online. Made you think you were losing it."

The plane lurches over a patch of rough air in our descent, and I'm suddenly nauseous. What he's saying can't be true.

"Go on." He motions toward the flight deck phone. "Ask her."

CHAPTER TEN

THERE'S NO WAY *Becca would do that. I know her.*

I meet Mitch's cold gaze, my eyes narrowing. "You still haven't told me who you really are and why you've been stalking me." I reach for the radio transmit button. "I'm calling the ground authorities to arrest you when we land."

Mitch's calm voice comes through my headset. "Go ahead. But I'm afraid with your history, making outlandish false accusations about another pilot will likely end your career."

My teeth clench as I absorb his words, knowing he might be right.

"I'm a First Officer for Vantage Skies. My full name is Mitchell Ortiz. And I'm jump seating back to Seattle, where I live. Happy? Now..." Mitch leans forward, bringing his face beside my headrest. "If you want to know what happened to the captain, I'm afraid you'll have to ask Becca, the first-class flight attendant."

I glance at the moving map display, which shows the descent point for 18,000 feet quickly approaching. If I don't ask Becca now, I won't have another chance until after we're on the ground. How did Mitch know that Becca tried to convince me he couldn't be the guy I met online? I think back to the other night at my house, when Becca discouraged me from calling the police. Is it possible she could've poisoned the captain? But why?

I cut my eyes toward Mitch. His biceps strain against his sleeves. The muscles I once found attractive are now nothing but a threat. I throw him a warning look, but he meets it with that same infuriating calm.

I pick up the flight attendant handset and press the call button, assured at least that Mitch isn't packing a gun. If his plan were to take over the flight deck, he could've done it already. Becca picks up on the third ring.

"Becca? It's Claire. Can you come up to the flight deck for a minute?"

A pause.

"I know it's breaking protocol to open the flight deck door, but I have to talk to you."

"Um. Okay. Just a sec."

Mitch leans forward, and my whole body tenses from his proximity. "Do you really think that's a good idea, inviting someone who might have poisoned Rob onto the flight deck?"

A tone sounds as a light on the center console glows. Someone has typed in the code to enter the flight deck. Still holding the handset, I say, "It's Claire."

"Golf ball." Becca responds with the code word for the day we had discussed earlier for flight deck entry.

I twist the unlock switch, and an audible *click* follows. Turning in my seat, I pull my left headphone behind my ear.

Becca's eyes are red from crying; she's clearly distraught over what's happened to Rob. "Rob still has no pulse, but they're giving him CPR. What is it?" She asks after the door locks behind her.

Mitch assesses the flight attendant expectantly. I narrow my eyes at him as a surge of anger races through my veins. Anger at myself for allowing this man to make me suspect my best friend of murder.

It suddenly strikes me that I might've fallen for a trap. What if he's planning to kill us both? The only crew left would be Tony and Nova, and he'd have full control of the flight deck. I study the smug look on Mitch's face. I have no idea what his motives are. For all I know, this could be an act of terror. Stalking me could've been a means to taking down the plane. It's an extreme suspicion, but fear has a way of making extremes feel real. And if I'm right, I've stupidly broken protocol by taking his bait.

I turn to Becca, needing to get her out of here. "Sorry, Bec. It's nothing that can't wait." Rain beats against the windscreen as we continue to descend over Illinois. "I know you have your hands full back there. You better get back."

"Actually, Becca." Mitch extends his arm, blocking her path to the door. "Claire and I were wondering if you could clear something up for us. You see, Claire doesn't seem to think you're capable of poisoning the captain. Even though I've assured her it was you who slipped the drug into Rob's coffee."

Becca shoots me a frightened look.

"There's no point in denying it, Becca," Mitch adds. "I know it was you."

Becca's hand trembles as she looks between Mitch and me, her eyes wide. She's clearly rattled by Mitch's accusation, like she knows something isn't right up here. It makes me regret my decision even more to bring her onto the flight deck.

"Becca, I want you to return to the cabin," I say, working to sound authoritative rather than panicked. I'm not sure what Mitch is doing. Whatever it is, I've played right into his hand.

Mitch lowers his arm, and I exhale in relief. But instead of turning for the door, Becca chokes out a sob, lifting her tortured gaze to mine.

"I'm sorry, Claire. But I didn't have a choice."

CHAPTER ELEVEN

"Becca." I gape at my friend in confusion. "What are you talking about? Didn't have a choice in what?"

A male voice comes over the radio. "Cascadia three two three, descend and maintain one-zero, ten thousand, Peoria altimeter two niner eight seven."

I remain turned in my seat, willing my friend to tell me she had nothing to do with Rob's death. That she's referring to something else. Beside her, a grin spreads across Mitch's handsome face, making my stomach sink.

"It was Steven," Becca says, her watery eyes locking with mine. "He made me do it. I didn't have a choice."

"Made you do what, Becca?" I stare at her in disbelief. There's no way my friend of ten years could be capable of murder.

Her chin quivers. "I slipped the capsule in Rob's coffee. Steven told me it was a sedative—no one was supposed to get hurt! It was only supposed to put Rob to sleep. I—" Her voice breaks into another sob. *"It wasn't supposed to kill him!"* She puts her hands on her head and dips her head toward the floor. "Oh, God. What have I done?"

My stomach churns. I think I'm going to throw up.

"Cascadia three two three, Chicago Center, descend and maintain one zero, ten thousand, Peoria altimeter three zero zero eight."

Mitch gestures to the controls. "Do you need some help? I can—"

"No," I snap. "Stay where you are." My mind whirls with questions as I press the radio transmit button. "Cascadia three two three, roger, descending to one-zero, ten thousand." I dial 10000 in the altitude window of the mode control panel. The thrust levers slowly retard as the airplane begins a gradual descent. I turn back around. Becca lifts her head, and I glare at her. "So, you're in on this? Whatever this is?" I point to Mitch. "With *him?*"

Becca shakes her head. "I'm not in on anything. I was only doing what Steven told me to." She motions toward the jump seat pilot. "I lied. I haven't flown with him before, but Nova has, and the rumor is he's on probation for losing his temper with a flight attendant."

Mitch frowns as Becca continues.

"Steven sent me his picture and told me to convince you to get on that dating app and encourage you to go out with him after he sent you a match request." She cringes. "I'm so sorry, Claire. But I don't know anything else about him or what the hell's going on." Becca swipes a tear from her cheek.

I study my best friend, still in shock that she would've done such a thing. I recall her swiping my phone from my hands after I downloaded the app, wanting to see all the guys who'd sent me a match request. How she'd gushed over "Evan's" profile, joking that if I didn't go out with him, she would go in my place.

Do I even know her at all? And why would Steven go to the trouble of all this? I've known him to be heartless, but manipulating my best friend into murder was beyond anything I believed him capable of. "How did Steven get you to do it?"

Becca shoots Mitch a wary glance.

"Go ahead, Becca," he says. "Steven already told me everything."

Becca then fixes her gaze on the windscreen, avoiding my eyes. "Years ago, right after you and I met, I'd gone out with some friends. We'd had a few drinks. I shouldn't have been driving, but my apartment was only a couple of miles from the bar. It was raining, and..." Becca swallows, fresh tears brimming her eyes. "I hit a cyclist. A man. It happened so fast. I tried to stop but...Then, I panicked. When I got out of the car, I was sure the man was dead—that there was nothing I could do for him. He was lying face down on the road, one of his legs out at this horrific angle, and his bike was crumpled like a bent paperclip." She shifts her gaze to the ceiling. "I was so scared. I wasn't thinking clearly. If I'd thought there was a chance to save him, I never would have left."

Her eyes seem to plead with mine when she lowers her gaze, but I'm unable to sympathize with her.

"My nose was broken from hitting the steering wheel," Becca continues. "It wouldn't stop bleeding. So, I drove to an ER in the next town over, saying I'd hit a deer with my car. It was when Steven was doing his ER rotation of his surgical residency. He was the doctor who treated me and said I also had a concussion. When Steven pressed me, saying that alcohol can mimic or worsen head trauma, I admitted to having a few drinks. They took my blood, but I didn't know Steven had ordered a tox screen until later. Steven saw the police bulletin that night about the hit-and-run involving the cyclist and took photos of my damaged car in the parking lot. The cyclist survived but lost one of his legs. Steven texted the pictures to me the next day, along with a copy of my tox screen showing I was over the legal limit, saying he knew what I'd done, but that he would keep my secret."

A female voice emanates over the radio. "Cascadia three two three, contact Chicago Center on one two four point eight."

I dial the new frequency into the radio panel. "Cascadia three two three, roger. Chicago Center on one two four point eight." I study Becca as though she were a stranger. How could she have kept this from me all this time?

"He brought it up again a couple of weeks ago. Told me if I didn't get you on the app and slip a sedative into the captain's drink, he'd send the evidence of my hit-and-run to the police."

Becca takes in my obvious revulsion, and her eyes fill with tears. "I had no choice, Claire. If Steven sent those photos and my lab report to the police, I'd lose everything: my job, my kids, my freedom. I'd be going to prison! I wouldn't see my kids grow up. I don't have to tell you what a monster Steven can be—you know what he's like."

A male voice crackles over the radio. "Cascadia three two three, Chicago Center, are you on frequency?"

"Did you ever stop to think why Steven wanted you to drug Rob, and what might happen to everyone else on this plane if you *drugged the captain?*"

A cry escapes Becca's mouth as her shoulders heave. "I'm so sorry."

My mind reels from Becca's confession as I recall the night of my car accident. I left my purse containing my Clonazepam downstairs while Olivia showed me her dollhouse. Steven made my tea. He must've slipped pills into my drink, which explains why I don't remember taking them. Just like he got Becca to slip the drug into Rob's coffee.

My throat wells with emotion. All this time, I've blamed myself, thought I was responsible for nearly killing my daughter. But it was Steven. It had to be. He not only endangered me that night, but our daughter. We both could've died. And he did it anyway. *Is that what he hoped would happen?* Kill us both off so he could look like a victim to his friends and family, then start fresh? A new family, perhaps. A clean slate. Just the thought makes me want to puke.

"You were right, Claire," Mitch says.

I turn to see he's taken off his shoulder harnesses, and he's watching Becca calmly. *What is his part in this?* I wonder. *And how did Steven get to him?*

"I *have* been stalking you since our date. Your ex-husband hired me to make you look unstable—not too difficult with someone like you. Your going to the police last night to report a phantom stalker will only help things."

"Cascadia three two three, Chicago Center, are you on frequency?" the controller asks again.

"Cascadia three two three affirmative," I respond.

The controller responds immediately. "Cascadia three two three, cross NINIC at one zero, ten thousand and contact St. Louis Approach on one two five point eight."

"Cascadia three two three roger, cross NINIC at one zero, ten thousand, St. Louis on one two five point eight," I reply before turning back to Becca.

She swipes another tear from her cheek with the back of her hand. "I can't believe Rob is dead. This is all my fault."

Yes, it is, I think. And Steven's. "This is much more than a medical emergency, and the ground authorities need to know." I pull my headphones over my ears as Mitch gives me a twisted smile.

"Your word against ours. And with your mental health history? They won't believe you."

Becca shifts her gaze from Mitch's face to mine, guilt clouding her eyes. "I'll tell the police everything as soon as we land."

At this, Mitch jerks his head up. "You can't do that."

But it's like she can't hear him at all. "All of it. My hit-and-run, and how Steven blackmailed me and put me up to poisoning the captain. I promise." Her lower lip trembles. "I should've come forward a long time ago."

Mitch unbuckles and stands, moving toward her. "You'll keep your mouth shut."

My body tenses as Becca takes a step back. Before I can react, Mitch grabs the fire extinguisher. A hollow, metallic *clunk* reverberates through the flight deck when Mitch slams the extinguisher into the side of Becca's head. She falls to the floor, unconscious, her head landing on the center console beside my seat. Blood seeps from a gash in her temple.

I gasp. Mitch stands over her, crouching beneath the short ceiling while holding the extinguisher with Becca's blood smeared on the bottom. I whip around, looking for some-thing—anything—to fight back with as I reach for the radio transmit button. Before I can get a word out, Mitch wraps my shoulder harness around my neck and pulls it taut.

CHAPTER TWELVE

GASP FOR AIR and grope at the harness around my neck. Mitch pulls it tighter, leaving no room for me to get a finger beneath the strap as my throat closes in on itself.

"Cascadia three two three, contact Chicago Center, if you hear, contact St. Louis approach on one two eight point eight," comes over the radio.

I grunt as pressure builds in my head, and I'm no longer able to move any air into my lungs. Gripped with panic, I swing my arms frantically behind me. My fist connects with Mitch's cheek. He lets out a groan before pulling the strap tighter. The fabric cuts into my neck, and my vision blurs. I take another swing at him, but he's leaned the other way, and I hit only air.

Mitch's voice sounds through my headphones. "It's a shame you killed the captain and tried to crash the plane while having a psychotic break. It's leaving me no choice. You even killed your best friend when she tried to stop you. She'd been so worried about your mental health."

Stars fill my vision. My head feels like it might explode.

The control panel blurs. I reach for the radio transmit button and press it, but I'm unable to make any noise aside from a grunt.

"Fortunately," Mitch says into my headset, "I was here to kill you in self-defense and land the plane a hero. Plus, I'll be getting a hefty payment from your ex."

I grit my teeth, forcing myself to stay conscious as I scan the control panel for something I can use as a weapon. I blink, trying in vain to clear my waning vision as I claw at the strap cutting into my neck.

Mitch brings his face closer to mine and speaks into his mic. "Sounds like your daughter will be better off with your ex anyway."

Anger ignites under my skin, along with a flash of adrenaline. I think of Olivia being raised solely by Steven, the monster responsible for the car accident that could have killed us both. Using every ounce of energy I have left, I disconnect the autopilot and turn the yoke all the way to the left.

The plane lurches, rolling past ninety degrees. The horizon spins across the windscreen, my stomach twisting with it, until we're completely upside down. I push forward on the yoke, fighting to keep the nose from diving straight toward the ground.

Mitch falls onto the overhead panel. His back hits the hydraulic switches, causing several yellow lights to illuminate on the overhead and forward instrument panels. Becca's body lands on top of him. I clutch my throat, gasping for air as the noose loosens around my neck and blood returns to my head. I rip the shoulder strap away from me.

The autopilot disconnect alarm wails, muffling the

controller's voice coming over the radio. "Cascadia three two three, I show you five-hundred feet low, check altitude."

A loud tone sounds as the ALT ALERT light flashes on the forward instrument panel. I keep pushing forward on the control yoke, knowing that I must keep the nose of the airplane above the horizon for there to be any hope of recovering.

I'm suspended upside down by my seatbelt, my vision starry, and I strain to stay conscious. Out the windshield, green farmlands sprawl past, the earth where the sky should be. Beneath me, Becca lies limp on top of Mitch. With a groan, Mitch shoves her against the bulkhead. He gets to his knees and wraps his hands around my throat. I run my hand along the wall behind my seat until my fingers find the crash axe. I grip the metal and tear it from the wall.

I turn toward Mitch who's seething through clenched teeth as he chokes me. "You bitch."

I swing the crash axe into the side of his neck with all my might. His hands go limp around my neck as his eyes roll toward the top of his head. He falls backward, landing beside Becca, who remains unmoving.

I lower my gaze to the windscreen. The nose is pointed below the horizon, and we're plummeting toward the ground. I cough, throat on fire. Hanging upside down this long makes my pulse pound in my temples from the blood rushing to my head. I fight to stay awake, mustering all the energy I can, knowing if I pass out, everyone dies.

With all my strength, I turn the yoke to the far right, but the airplane is slow to respond. Something is wrong with the controls—they feel extremely heavy, like they're set in concrete. I shift my gaze to the overhead panel. An amber LOW PRESSURE light is illuminated above all four hydraulic pressure switches. Mitch must've accidentally flipped them off when he landed on the panel.

The nose dips farther as I reach beside his neck, pushing his head to the side to get to the switches. His shoulder rolls onto my hand from the steep angle of the floor before I can switch them on.

"Ahh!" I shove his shoulder a few inches to the side, forcing his body against Becca's. My hand shakes as I barely manage to flip the four switches back to ON before his body rolls onto my hand again.

The plane starts to respond, but the nose is still pointed too low, and we're plummeting toward the earth. Using both hands, I tug the yoke all the way to right, ignoring the screeching alarm and the loud robotic voice screaming, "terrain, terrain—pull up," repeatedly through the flight deck speakers. As the plane rolls through ninety degrees, I change from pushing forward to pulling back, but the nose dips farther. Becca, still unconscious, falls into the captain's seat beside me as Mitch's body hits the floor, slamming against the back of the seat. My heart rises into my throat as the farmlands loom at a nauseating ninety degrees, growing closer and closer in the windscreen.

Even with the hydraulics back on, I might be too late.

CHAPTER THIRTEEN

"**S**HIT."

The airplane is pointed almost straight down while our airspeed is increasing. I pull the yoke in toward my chest. If I can't get the nose up before the airplane gains speed, the G-forces from pulling out of the dive will break the plane apart. But if I don't pull hard enough, we'll hit the ground.

My body feels like a sack of concrete, pinned to my seat by the pull of the G load. Blood drains from my head from the force of gravity. My vision dims to gray, a pilot's warning sign of an approaching black out, when the Gs starve the eyes of blood. I let out a loud grunt, forcing air into my upper body—the technique I was taught during my aerobatic training to keep from blacking out during high-G maneuvers.

"Ahh!" I pull the yoke harder against my torso, lifting the nose as our altitude drops so low I can now trace the lines of the cornfields below, every row etched into the earth.

I breathe deep, raking air into my lungs as I work to level off when the nose lifts above the horizon. I glance at Becca, who remains slumped over the captain's seat. After starting a shallow climb, I rest a hand on Becca's back.

"Thank God," I mutter, feeling the subtle rise and fall of her breathing. She was wrong to do what she did, but she doesn't deserve to die from it.

A change on the fuel indicator catches my eye. My relief that the plane didn't break apart evaporates when I see the fuel indication has turned from white to amber, and the word LOW appears in yellow below the fuel indicators. The fuel numbers on both wing tanks are rapidly dropping.

My body goes rigid, knowing we only have a few minutes before the engines flame out. I punch the radio transmit button. "Cascadia three two three, I need an airport within seven or eight minutes. I have a rapid fuel leak." *Something must have ruptured in the wing fuel tanks from the G forces.*

"Cascadia three two three, this is Chicago Center. Your closest airport is still Peoria, Papa India Alpha, two five miles at your twelve o'clock."

I close my eyes, sinking back against my seat. "Cascadia, three two three. Negative, that's too far. My engines will flame out before then. I need a closer option."

"Cascadia three two three, that's your closest option, other than some small private dirt strips."

I assess the farm fields below as my heart thuds against my ribs. There's no way we're making it to a runway. "Cascadia, three two three, we'll be landing in a corn field."

"Cascadia, roger." The controller's words come faster, edged with stress. "I'll notify the local emergency services to be standing by. Let me know if I can be of any further assistance."

I turn my attention to the controls. I need to get the

landing gear and flaps down before the engines flame out. It will be much safer to land while we still have some power available than to do a "dead stick" landing. But there isn't much time. A moan emits from either Becca or Mitch, but I have no time to check which one it came from. After the axe to the neck, I don't know how he could still be alive.

I fix my gaze on a long green field in the distance straight ahead where the terrain looks relatively flat. I pull the gear lever down to decrease our speed and begin lowering the flaps, aware that the engines could flame out at any second.

I grab the PA microphone. "Flight attendants, prepare for crash landing."

I use the engines to slow our rate of descent as we soar toward the corn field.

"Please don't flame out," I mumble, watching the fuel indicators approaching zero.

I glance at the altimeter as we pass below 2500 feet. Out the corner of my eye, I spot Becca's seat belt dangling loose over the side of her seat. She should have it on, but with one hand on the yoke and the other on the thrust levers, there's nothing I can do about it now.

The numbers on the digital readout slowly decrease as we drop below 1,000 feet. The cornfield ahead is now clearer, resolving into sharp green lines. I rest one hand on the thrust levers, keeping my gaze fixed on the field below.

A computerized voice calls out "five hundred" over the speakers.

I bring the PA mic toward my mouth. *"Brace, brace, brace!"*

We drop below one hundred feet, then the same voice shouts, "fifty, forty, thirty, twenty, ten." I ease the thrust levers to idle and pull back on the yoke to hold the nose up as long as possible. I hold my breath as the plane hits the field.

The nose slams down, the wheels gouging into the soft soil. The jolt whips me forward in my harness, the straps digging into my shoulders and chest. My teeth cut into my lip, and I taste blood as corn stalks and dirt explode against the windscreen, blotting out the world. My lungs heave against the harness as we plow through the corn at a hundred thirty miles per hour. Becca pitches forward, her body slamming into the yoke. Mitch's legs smack hard against the base of the center console.

A corn cob splinters the window with a sharp *crack*. I gasp as the deceleration whiplashes Becca and me in our seats. Becca cries out. Then, abruptly, the wall of cornstalks vanishes, the windscreen flooding with blue sky and sunlight. Instinctively, I stand on the brakes as we glide over a grassy area, which does nothing to slow our speed. The landing gear must have collapsed. There's nothing else I can do except hang on as we barrel toward a weathered red barn.

We skid atop a patch of gravel, our speed slowing. The structure looms closer. I clamp my fingers around the yoke, every muscle braced for impact. Becca tries to sit up, then screams as the nose crashes through the side of the barn. Wood splinters against the windscreen before we come to a stop inside the barn.

My head smacks against my headrest as I peer through the cracked windscreen at the barn, which is thankfully empty. Light shines through a hole on the opposite wall where siding is missing.

I slip off my headphones and turn to Becca. "Are you okay?"

Her chest heaves with her rapid breathing as she pushes off the seat and stares out the windscreen. The blood on her temple from where Mitch hit her with fire extinguisher is now smeared down her cheek.

"Becca?"

"What happened?" She shakily unbuckles her seatbelt and sits upright. Seeing Mitch, and the axe lodged in the base of his neck, she shrieks.

"We crash landed," I say, putting the fuel levers to cutoff in hopes of avoiding a fire. "I'll tell you the rest later."

Becca gapes at Mitch while I reach for the PA microphone. *"Evacuate, evacuate, evacuate."*

I lower the PA, and for half a breath, I can't move. We're alive. Against all odds, I managed to put us down in one piece. My disbelief morphs to gratitude as I'm suddenly aware of the countless ways this could've ended in our deaths.

After I replace the PA mic, Becca shakily gets to her feet. "I'll go help Tony and Nova get the passengers out." She covers her mouth with her hand as she steps over Mitch.

While Becca leaves the flight deck, the air traffic controller's voice crackles through my headset around my neck. "Cascadia three two three, how do you read, over?"

I slide my headset back on, amazed the radio is still working. "This is Cascadia three two three. We've landed in a corn field and require immediate medical assistance."

"Roger, emergency response teams are enroute to you now. Nice work getting that plane safely on the ground."

I unbuckle and slip off my headset before climbing out of my seat. Mitch is lying on his stomach, unmoving. I shudder and lift my gaze as Becca appears in the door to the flight deck.

"Claire, are you coming?"

"Yeah, I'm coming. What's the status?"

"Some got pretty banged up, but all the passengers are alive."

I exhale, leaning back against my seat. "Good. What about Rob?"

Becca's eyes brim with tears as she shakes her head. She brings a hand to her forehead as a sob escapes her mouth. My throat swells with emotion, grief twisting into anger at Steven for orchestrating this, and at Mitch and Becca for playing their parts. Guilt needles at me—if it weren't for me, Rob would still be alive—but I shove it down. This wasn't my doing. It was theirs.

I climb out of my seat. "Let's go help get everyone off."

Becca turns, and I see first class is empty. The remaining passengers on board are lined up in the aisle, making their way toward the middle and rear exits.

Tony and Nova are shouting instructions near the back, directing passengers to leave their luggage behind and to tuck their arms before going down the slide. I'm about to follow Becca out of the flight deck when Mitch's leg bumps against my ankle. I stop, looking down to find his leg twitching. I slide my gaze up his body. His chest rises and falls ever so slightly with shallow breaths.

I suck in a sharp breath. *He's alive.*

EPILOGUE

Six Weeks Later

"HIGHER, MOMMY," OLIVIA calls out after I give her back a gentle shove on the swing set.

She swings backward, and I push harder. She soars forward with a squeal of delight. With Steven in prison, I've been awarded full custody of Olivia, and we've been making the most of our time together when I'm not working. We discovered this park, less than a mile from our house, a few weeks ago and have come every day it hasn't been raining.

"When will Grandma get here?" Olivia asks.

"Not until after dinner, but she'll be with you for the three nights I'm gone for work."

Aside from a blond-haired boy who's climbing up the slide from the bottom, Olivia is the only child in the park on this surprisingly clear day in November. I gaze at the boy's young mother bundled up in a puffy down coat sitting on the park bench scrolling through her phone.

Her auburn ponytail reminds me of Becca, who's currently serving out a twelve-year sentence at a federal prison over an hour away. I feel a jab in my chest over Becca's betrayal mixed with sadness at how many precious moments like this my longtime friend will miss out on for the rest of her boys' childhood.

The drone of a jet engine causes me to lift my gaze. I shield my eyes from the afternoon sun with my hand as the belly of a Cascadia airliner flies over us, taking my mind back to that disastrous flight.

After Becca gave a full confession to the FBI and I gave my statement about everything that happened on the flight deck, the FBI found Steven's communication with Mitch on Mitch's phone.

Steven was arrested soon after. He vehemently proclaimed his innocence until his attorney convinced him there was too much evidence, along with Becca's confession, for Steven to have a chance at convincing a jury of being not guilty. A week later, after Mitch woke up from a medically induced coma, he told the police everything. After being placed on probation for his outburst at the flight attendant, Mitch went to see Steven as a patient, hoping to get carpal tunnel surgery out of the way in case he was fired and lost his health insurance.

When Mitch admitted to Steven that he wasn't sure he could afford the deductible for his procedure due to drowning in gambling debts and being on the brink of losing his home, Steven made Mitch an offer. He proposed a plan to salvage Mitch's reputation by deeming him a hero, along with a hefty financial payment.

After Mitch's confession, Steven pled guilty, taking a plea deal in exchange for some of his many charges being dropped and to avoid the spectacle of trial. While Steven may have avoided what he felt would've been an even bigger blow to his ego, he was still sentenced to life imprisonment along with Mitch.

In the end, Steven confessed to everything. Well, almost everything. He never admitted to drugging my tea with my Clonazepam, even though I'm certain now that he did.

He did admit, however, to hacking into my email to find my flight schedule. Afterward, the FBI discovered that Steven's IP address had hacked into my email several times since our separation, which was how he deleted the email notifying me of our custody hearing. He'd even replied to himself from my account, agreeing to pick up Olivia from school before deleting the email thread from my inbox so I would look like an unfit parent who was losing her mind.

While I've visited Becca in prison, I haven't taken Olivia to visit Steven. And I'm not sure that I ever will, until she's old enough to understand and decide for herself.

Olivia bounds off the swing through the air, drawing me back to the present as she lands on her feet. She whirls around to face me, her wide grin exposing her missing front tooth.

"Can we play tag, Mommy?"

I return her smile. "Sure, sweetie."

She rushes toward me, slapping me on the leg as she moves past. "You're it. No tag backs!"

I chase after her, drawing in a breath of cool air as it strikes me how lucky I am to be here. If Steven had his way, I wouldn't be. And possibly, neither would Olivia. I run after her, closing the gap between us as Olivia's long hair whips behind her from the breeze. I lift her off the ground in a swift motion. Olivia shrieks before I plant a kiss on her cheek.

"Got you."

Keep reading for a sample of
Audrey J. Cole's locked-room thriller,

MISSING IN FLIGHT!

CHAPTER ONE

MAKAYLA

Present

THE WEIGHT OF her head bobbing to the side jars Makayla awake. The cabin is dark. She tilts her head to stretch her neck, suddenly aware of the sharp ache in her bladder. She's still wearing her wrap, but when she looks down, Liam is no longer against her chest. Panic rises to her throat. Her gaze snaps to the bassinet against the bulkhead wall, and she remembers laying Liam down before drifting off to sleep.

She leans forward and exhales, seeing the outline of his sleeping form. He's hardly moved since she last checked on him. She sinks against her seat, still in its upright position, and unbuckles her seat belt.

A glance at her phone tells her there's nearly five hours to go. She bites her lip as she looks at Liam. There's no way she can hold it that long.

I should've gone before we boarded. Sitting forward, she considers putting Liam back into the wrap and taking him with her to the lavatory. His pacifier lies beside him. She can't imagine getting him back to sleep after waking him with the fluorescent lavatory lights and loud suction of the toilet flushing. Just yesterday, after she'd finally gotten Liam to sleep by taking him for a stroller walk along the downtown Anchorage harbor, a tugboat blared its horn and woke him, and she had to deal with his screaming for the next twenty minutes. She hates to disturb him while he's adjusting to the time change. In New York, waking him now might even undo his new sleep pattern. If he sleeps through the rest of the flight, he'll be back on his New York schedule.

Makayla leans into the aisle and looks around the cabin, which is quiet aside from the drone of the engines. The few passengers around her are asleep, except for the college-aged girl across the aisle who's engrossed in what looks to be a thriller playing on the in-flight video screen. Makayla reaches up and presses the flight attendant call button. Surely, one of them wouldn't mind standing by Liam for the few minutes it takes her to use the bathroom.

The minutes feel like hours as she waits for someone to come. Makayla presses her lips together, trying to think of anything besides how bad she has to pee. Hearing voices in the cabin behind her, she peers down the aisle. A male and a female flight attendant are helping an elderly woman back to her seat. Makayla recognizes the petite, white-haired passenger as the woman an airline employee had to assist onto the plane when she and Liam boarded.

The plane bounces from a bout of turbulence. Makayla inhales a sharp breath from the jolt to her full bladder as the flight attendants struggle to keep the woman from falling over.

"Let go of me!" As the elderly passenger jerks away from one of the attendants, she loses her balance.

Makayla pities the woman, who, from the look of confusion and fear in her eyes, has some sort of dementia. She faces forward in her seat, knowing those two flight attendants won't be answering her call anytime soon. But maybe there is another in the rear galley that could watch over Liam for a few minutes. *Although,* she thinks, *by the time I find someone to come watch over Liam, I could just use the lavatory.*

After checking that Liam is still asleep, Makayla stands. She looks to the young woman across the aisle, who she recognizes from the boarding area, and taps her on the shoulder. The young woman lifts her head toward Makayla, making no effort to pull back her bright-pink headphones.

"Excuse me." Makayla leans toward her. "Would you mind listening for my baby while I use the bathroom?" She points to the bassinet, then the back of the plane. "He's asleep, and I'll be right back. There's a pacifier lying next to him if he wakes up."

The girl glances in the direction of the rear lavatory before nodding. "Yeah."

"Oh, thank you." Makayla offers a smile, and the girl returns to her in-flight entertainment.

After getting the elderly woman to her seat, the flight attendants retreat behind the lavatories as Makayla hurries down the aisle. A cold hand encircles her wrist when Makayla passes the older woman's row. Makayla gasps and yanks away, freeing her hand from the woman's grip.

The woman holds a trembling hand toward Makayla. "Sarah, is that you? They won't tell me where Roger is. Have you seen him?"

"I'm so sorry," a tall blond flight attendant says to Makayla before stepping in between her and the elderly woman. The small diamond stud in the side of her nose reminds Makayla of her friend Cori, a new mother Makayla met before the start of the summer.

The old woman unbuckles her seat belt and shakily stands.

"Rose, I need you to stay in your seat." The attendant's voice takes on a firm tone as Rose makes an unsteady attempt for the aisle.

Makayla continues toward the lavatory as a male flight attendant, short and slightly pudgy, strides down the aisle from the rear of the plane.

"You need some help there, Britt?" he asks.

Makayla steps to the side for him to pass by her, reading the name she heard him being called when he came by earlier with the drink cart. It was pinned to his navy sweater-vest: *Derek.* Before opening the door to the lavatory, Makayla looks beyond the two flight attendants to her seat at the front of the cabin. There's no movement or sound coming from Liam's bassinet. The girl with the pink headphones turns in his direction before looking back at her screen.

Makayla steps inside the small bathroom, feeling a pang of guilt for leaving her baby in the hands of a stranger.

Liam's fine, she reassures herself. Words from the therapist she saw after her mother died pop into her mind as she unzips her jeans. *You should never feel guilty for taking care of your own needs.*

When she sits on the toilet, she feels almost instant relief, knowing her therapist was right. *This will only take a minute. And Liam won't even know I was gone.*

After drying her hands, Makayla tucks a strand of hair that's fallen loose from her ponytail behind her ear and wipes away a small smear of mascara from beneath her eye. She unlocks the lavatory door and pushes on it. The lights flicker inside the small space, but the door doesn't budge. Stemming her impulse to panic, she uses both hands to press her weight into the door. It opens with an audible crack.

From his seat across the aisle, Derek, the flight attendant, meets Makayla's gaze when she steps out of the lavatory. She averts her eyes, shaking the uncomfortable sensation of the male attendant's stare as she emerges from the bathroom. Spotting the side of Liam's bassinet, she takes a deep breath, feeling the tension dissipate from her shoulders. *He's fine.*

Taking quick steps down the narrow aisle, keeping her arms close to her sides, Makayla passes the row where the elderly woman is eating from a tiny bag of pretzels and calmly watching an episode of *Friends* on the seat-back screen in front of her. Makayla contains a smile.

In the next row, a retirement-age couple appears to be asleep, the woman's head on the man's shoulder. Makayla thinks of Jack, wishing he could've come with them.

When she nears the bulkhead, her eyes are drawn to the screen of the young woman across from her, showing a car's headlights speeding down a gravel road at night. She touches the girl on the arm before sitting down.

"Thank you."

The girl looks up, keeping her headphones on. "Sure."

The girl refocuses on her screen as Makayla turns for her

seat. She stops. Her heart somersaults. Mouth open and eyes wide, she steps toward Liam's bassinet.

An airplane pillow lies in the place of her son, tucked into his blanket. She snatches the pillow, lifting it into the air as she spins around. Her eyes dart to the young woman's lap as she lifts a pop can toward her mouth. Makayla yanks the pink headphones off the girl's head. Her soda sloshes out from the can.

"Where's my son?"

She lifts a startled gaze to Makayla. "Whoa! What are you doing?"

Makayla points to the empty bassinet. "My *son*. Where is he?"

The girl's eyes train on the direction of Makayla's finger. Her brows knit together as she gapes at Makayla's actions. "I—I don't know."

Makayla scans the sleeping passengers around them. "I asked you to watch him."

The girl's confused expression melts into irritation. "I thought you were asking if the bathroom was in the back." She takes her headphones from Makayla's grip.

Makayla clutches the pillow to her chest. "But where is he? Who took him?"

The girl glances at the bassinet. "I . . . I don't know."

"Well, *someone* took him out of there." How could the girl not have seen a stranger plucking him out of the bassinet?

"I didn't see anyone." She stares blankly at Makayla. "I was watching a movie."

Makayla whips around, inspecting each sleeping passenger's lap for a sign of her baby.

"Excuse me," she calls, moving up the aisle. "Has anyone

seen my son? My baby. I just went to the bathroom, and he's gone."

A few passengers open their eyes and shake their heads. Makayla is almost to the lavatories in the middle of the plane, and there's no sign of Liam. She hurries toward the crew seat behind the bathroom, only to find it empty. She scans the rear cabin for someone holding Liam, but the spaced-out passengers all look to be asleep or engrossed in their screens. And she can't see Derek anywhere.

Makayla turns. A few passengers have gotten up from their seats. Makayla recognizes two of them as the retirement-age couple she passed on her way back from the lavatory, and the other as the petite dark-haired woman who handed her Liam's pacifier when they boarded. As her husband bumped into Makayla from behind with their dog carrier. Now, the neatly dressed, muscular man remains seated.

"Did you see anyone come through here while I was in the bathroom?" Makayla asks.

"No," the man says.

The two women shake their heads. They each move up one of the aisles, scanning the rows for a sign of Liam.

"I didn't notice anyone besides the flight attendants helping that woman across from me," the dark-haired woman says.

The older woman stops and turns to Makayla from the aisle on the other side of the cabin, her expression twisted in bewilderment. "Sorry, I was asleep."

Makayla stands still, feeling the woman's eyes on her as the other two passengers reach the rear of their cabin. Not finding Liam, they turn toward Makayla, the alarm on their faces causing a spike in her anxiety.

The blond flight attendant emerges from business class,

making her way up the aisle on the other side of the plane. Makayla crosses through an empty middle row of seats and rushes toward the attendant, who stops close to Makayla's seat. When Makayla reaches her, the blond steps to the side, making room for Makayla to move past her.

"Excuse me." Makayla stops, aware of the panic in her voice. "I can't find my baby—my son. He's . . . he's not . . ." She exhales in frustration as her words fail to come out right. "Someone took him." She points to the empty bassinet affixed to the bulkhead wall.

Makayla thinks of Derek, now gone from his seat. *Please say that one of the crew has him. That he was crying while I was in the bathroom.* Instead, the attendant's eyebrows thread together beneath her bangs as she eyes the empty bassinet.

"Someone took him and put this in his place!" Makayla grabs the pillow and holds it inches from the attendant's face. *Why isn't she taking this more seriously?*

Pink Headphones gapes at Makayla, eyes wide.

"Okay, we'll find him. Try and stay calm." The attendant raises her hands, palms out, and Makayla recognizes it for what it is—an attempt to calm a difficult passenger. "I'll make an announcement. He can't be far."

"I don't understand. I was only gone for a couple of minutes."

"So, you weren't here?"

Makayla grips the top of the seat beside her and forces in a breath, but her lungs won't fully expand. "I just went to the bathroom. For like two minutes."

The woman's face relaxes. "Oh. Well, maybe someone tried to settle him while you were gone."

Makayla shakes her head. "He was asleep."

"Don't worry, I'll make an announcement."

"Can you turn on the lights?"

"Yes." The flight attendant turns and bumps into the woman who recovered Liam's pacifier when Makayla boarded.

The woman looks between Makayla and the attendant. "I moved up and down the cabin with another passenger. We didn't see your baby. Have you checked in first class?"

Makayla makes for the front of the aircraft, unsure if she responded to the woman trying to help her. The college-aged girl who was supposed to be watching Liam has resumed watching her movie beneath her pink headphones.

Makayla wants to shake her.

She flings the curtain open to business class, praying someone heard Liam crying and took him back to their seat when they couldn't find her. It's just as dark as the main cabin. In the three rows sectioned off by curtains at either end, Makayla spots only two passengers.

A middle-aged man wearing a suit sleeps with his head against the window. Makayla leans over and shakes him by the shoulder. His mouth closes with a snap as his eyes open.

"Hi, my baby . . . my baby, Liam, he was asleep in the bassinet right behind your seat in the main cabin. When I came back from the bathroom he was gone. Have you seen him?"

He shakes his head, eyes groggy. "No. Sorry."

A woman with a gray bob turns in her seat two rows in front of him. "Did you say you're looking for your baby?"

Makayla exhales with relief. She steps forward, hoping to find Liam in the older woman's lap. "Yes!"

Instead of Liam, the woman holds two knitting needles above a ball of yarn.

"I'm afraid there's been no baby up here, my dear," the woman says. "Did you check in the back?"

Makayla stares at the woman's lap and the empty seat beside her before yanking open the curtain to first class, scanning the few sleeping passengers and empty seats for a sign of Liam as she moves between the leather chairs.

Liam couldn't have been taken far—it's a plane. Plus, she wasn't in the lavatory for more than a few minutes. *How is this even possible?* Her lungs stiffen with fear, making it impossible to draw in a deep breath.

Where could he be? And why can't I find him?

AVAILABLE NOW

ABOUT THE AUTHOR

Audrey J. Cole is a USA TODAY bestselling thriller author, and her work has been translated into multiple languages. She resides in the Pacific Northwest with her two children. Before writing full time, she worked as a neonatal intensive care nurse for eleven years.

Sign up for her email list at www.audreyjcole.com to receive free bonus content, promotions, and new release updates.